sun moon stars rain

sun moon stars rain

Jan Cheripko

FRONT STREET
Asheville, North Carolina

For Peggy Wills,
who knows well the meaning
of "pass it on"

The lines from "anyone lived in a pretty how town"
Copyright © 1940, 1968, 1991 by the Trustees for the E. E. Cummings Trust,
from *Complete Poems: 1904–1962* by E. E. Cummings,
edited by George J. Firmage.
Used by permission of Liveright Publishing Corporation.

The lines from *Confessions of St. Augustine of Hippo*
Copyright © 1960, translated by John K. Ryan.
Image by Doubleday.

Copyright © 2006 by Jan Cheripko
All rights reserved
Designed by Helen Robinson
Printed in China

First edition

Library of Congress Cataloging-in-Publication Data
Cheripko, Jan.
Sun, moon, stars, rain / by Jan Cheripko. —1st ed.
p. cm.
ISBN 1-932425-53-5 (alk. paper)
[1. Interpersonal relations—Fiction. 2. Grief—Fiction.] I. Title.
PZ7.C41965Sun 2005
[Fic]—dc22

2005018170

Women and men(both little and small)
cared for anyone not at all
they sowed their isn't they reaped their same
sun moon stars rain

— *E. E. Cummings*
   from "anyone lived in a pretty how town"

sun moon stars rain

one

Ice.

Ice everywhere.

A morning stopped solid by ice.

Trees bent to the ground, defeated, bowed, humbled by a god of white war.

Ice.

Ice everywhere.

Thousands of

thousands of thousands

red, brown, black, gray,

reaching branches encased, immobilized, still, silhouetted, stretched out in homage to the conquering king.

Every step on his frozen carpet cracking like rocks smashing newborn diamonds; delicate movements through his brittle and pleading victims.

Ahead, guarding the entrance to his ancient kingdom of towering pine, hemlock, and firs, hangs heavy white mist, the living breath of the king, daring entrance to his realm.

Moments are made for mornings like this.

Movements, ideas, themes rise and fall, but moments attack.

I had just turned seventeen when I graduated from high

school. Pushed ahead in kindergarten. Now how do you figure that someone knows you're smart enough to skip a grade in kindergarten? Was my life made in that moment?

Or was it the moment at the age of six, when I sat at the piano in school and somehow music came out.

Moments on moments on moments on moments make up a life.

Frozen solid in ice.

two

"Hey!"

A quick turn, a foot grinding the frozen grass into the mud beneath it.

"Whaddaya doing?"

"Takin' some pictures," I say, holding up my camera to a grizzled, unshaven face only twenty feet away.

"You got permission?"

"No. Didn't know I needed any."

"That's a damned lie, and you know it, kid."

"Maybe," I mutter.

"Maybe, hell," says the man, walking closer. "The old man catches you in his woods, he'll shoot you, and then ask who the hell you are. So . . . ? Who the hell are you, anyway?"

"Danny. Danny Murtaugh."

"Humph! You're Danny Murtaugh? Chuck's boy?"

"Yeah."

"Well, I'll be damned. You were just a little kid last time I seen you," he says, now a few feet away. "Sorry 'bout your dad, boy."

"Yeah, well, it was a long time ago."

"S'pose. Didn't seem that long ago we was huntin' and fishin' these waters." He points to the river in the distance behind me. "Well, Danny Murtaugh, let me give you some good advice. You gonna get yourself shot, if you don't take care. You know as well as I do that this land—the trees, the river, all of it—belongs to Frederick P. Garrick, and he will shoot you."

"I appreciate the advice, Mr.—?"

"Samuels. Benjamin Samuels."

Benji Samuels. So this is the infamous Benji Samuels, the legend who comes out of the forest about once a month to stock up on a few groceries and lots of booze.

"Well, like I said, Mr. Samuels—"

"Benji. Most people call me Benji. Your dad did. Good enough for him, good enough for you."

"Well, Benji, I appreciate what you're sayin'. I just headed out this morning for a walk to get some photos of this ice storm. Kept walkin' and ended up here," I say, looking up at the ice-covered evergreens towering above us. "It's incredible. Just wanted some pictures."

Benji tilts his head back, his eyes sweeping in a long circle across the ice-coated deep green needles hanging on trunks of black jade. His head pivots back to position, eye-to-eye with me. He sighs heavy, and the smell of drink spoils the freshness of the woods.

"They are somethin' all right, aren't they? Some o' them big trees go back to when the Indians were here. That's the truth, you know. Never been cut. Never. All the rest around here," he says, swinging his arms wide and big, "everywhere, I mean everywhere, in this town, in this county, in this state, maybe even in the whole East Coast, they all been cut. But not these. There ain't no place on this godforsaken earth like this right here. All the trees you see everyplace else are all second growth, third growth. All hardwoods. They took all the big evergreens years, hell, centuries ago. Took 'em downriver to Philadelphia. They built the ships and the houses with them, and left nothin' behind. Nothin' but this. This escaped. And old Mr. Garrick, he ain't gonna let anybody, not even the state, take it. And that, too, is the truth."

It was true; everybody knew it. Frederick P. Garrick and the state had been fighting over his land for more than fifteen years. Why Garrick wouldn't sell was a puzzle. Most people figured it was because the state couldn't meet his price. They told him he had to sell. He said no. They tried to condemn the land. He fought back and is still fighting.

I can't resist asking. "Why doesn't he just sell the land? He'd make a ton of money. What's the big deal?"

"You don't know much, do you, kid? Your dad knew the answer to that. S'prised you don't. You sure you're Chuck's boy? He wudn't stupid."

"Sorry," I say sarcastically.

"You, you'd better be on your way. You're gonna get yourself shot."

I look around at the big trees surrounding us. A deep breath of cold air pings against my teeth and burns the inside of my chest. "Supposin' I asked Mr. Garrick for permission?"

"Permission for what?"

"To walk around these woods and take pictures."

Benji looks hard at me, and then he laughs.

"Yeah, you sure as hell are just like your dad, all right. He never took no for an answer, either. Go ahead, write him a letter."

"How about I just go and see him."

"Suit yourself, boy. But I'll tell you, he is inclined to shoot first. And that's the truth."

three

"Where've you been?" comes the question, hard and sharp, as I step in through the back door into the tiny kitchen.

"Out takin' pictures, " I mumble, trying to slip by her on the other side of the table.

"Don't track in mud on the floor."

That stops me.

"Take the boots off right there by the door. What time did you leave?"

" 'Bout six this morning," I say.

"Out since six this morning . . . ," she says.

"Yeah."

"Did it ever occur to you that this ice storm might have cut our power? No, I suppose it didn't occur to you," she says, answering her own question. "Well, our power is out. We don't have any electricity. No water. No heat. Nothing."

"Well, what do you want me to do about it?"

"I want you to take some responsibility around here. There isn't much to do about it now, but how would you know? You're not home."

"Mom, what do you want me to say? I'm sorry. I mean, I didn't even think about it."

"Didn't you notice that the lights weren't on this morning?"

"I didn't want to wake you, so I didn't turn any lights on."

"You didn't notice that it was cold?"

I shrug no.

She shakes her head, then says, "Billy's comin' over. He's bringin' a couple of kerosene heaters. It'll at least keep the pipes from freezin'. Let Jasper out, so he doesn't wet the rug."

"Come on, boy, out you go," I say, stroking Jasper's big golden head as he wags his whole body against my legs.

Jasper hits the leftover ice on the porch and sprawls into the air, all four legs spread, peeing all over the porch as he goes.

"My God, that is one talented dog you got there," calls Billy, stepping from his state park Jeep.

"Yeah, it took me months to teach him to do that," I shout back.

"I hope your mother . . . ," he says.

"'Your mother' what?" Mom hollers, opening the front door behind me. "Here," she says, handing me a mop and a bucket. "Clean the porch."

four

"Some ice storm, huh?" says Billy, licking his fingers, covered with the sticky icing of the cinnamon rolls that he brought.

When was it that Billy Taylor started visiting us? About eight years ago, a little more than a year after Dad died. Billy never tried to be "dad" to me. I wonder why Mom hasn't married him. Obviously, Billy likes her, and I guess she likes him, too, but is she ready to say good-bye to Dad, even though it's been nine years? I suppose not yet. Maybe if I had stayed in college, maybe then it would have been easier for her to move on, to marry Billy. Now that I'm home, she doesn't know what to do. And neither do I.

"Yep, some storm. 'Course, it shoulda been snow," says Billy. "We need snow bad. Here it is March, and we had only one big storm. What'd that drop, maybe three feet? Nothing besides that, and no real rain in the fall. This is one of the worst droughts I've ever seen. The city's main reservoir is down to almost 40 percent of capacity. We don't get some rain or snow soon, we're in for a long, long summer."

"We've had droughts before," says Mom, sorting through food in the refrigerator that might go bad if the electricity stays off.

"That's true," says Billy. "I remember that one eleven years ago.

First year I was out of college and went to work for the state. The only way we got out of that drought was the hurricane that came through in September. Difference was that we had a good snowfall the winter before. Not like this year. You remember it, Danny?"

"Not really. I was just a kid."

"You were seven," says Mom. "Two years before—" She doesn't finish the sentence.

Billy looks down into the last drops of his coffee, and I follow the cue.

"I went for a hike this morning," I say to Billy.

"Oh yeah?" says Billy.

"I thought I'd get some photos of this ice storm. It was beautiful. I ended up in Old Man Garrick's woods."

"What?" says Mom, turning around toward me. "You didn't tell me that!"

"You didn't let me."

Billy puts his empty cardboard coffee cup to his lips. "Quite a hike," he says, looking first at Mom, then me.

"What were you doin' way up there?" she asks.

"I don't know, just started walkin', and that's where I ended up."

"You're lucky you didn't get shot," she says.

"That's just what Benji Samuels told me."

"You ran into old Benji, huh?" says Billy.

"Yeah. He talked some about Dad. I guess I didn't realize they were close friends."

Billy looks up at Mom.

"Well, I wouldn't say they were close friends," she says, still looking at Billy. "They knew each other from school."

"Benji said they used to hunt and fish together."

"Well, hunting and fishing together doesn't mean they were good friends." She turns back to the food in the fridge. "They knew each other, that's all."

"No need to get upset, Mom. It's no big deal."

"I'm not upset. It's just that your father didn't hang around with drunken bums like Benji Samuels."

"Mom, really, there's no reason to get upset."

"What else did Benji have to say?" asks Billy, trying to change the subject.

"Not much," I say, with one last glance at Mom. "Just that those trees up there go back hundreds of years. I told him that I'm gonna get Garrick's permission to walk in his woods."

"What?" Mom says, turning to me.

"I'm gonna go see the old guy. I'll betcha he's not that bad."

"Billy, tell him Garrick's crazy. Tell him what you know about that man. He's crazy. Stay away from him."

"Well, he is strange, that much I know," says Billy. "He's been in court twelve times with the state over that land of his, and he's won every single time. He is one of the smartest men you'll ever meet and one of the most cantankerous, too. But he appreciates chutzpah. He just might give you permission—or he might shoot you."

five

"Mr. Garrick?"

Two gray eyes look out at me through silver-rimmed glasses. A bush of stringy, soft white hair hangs down around a wiry salt-and-pepper beard.

The old man says nothing, just stares from behind a half-opened front door as four big Rottweilers, penned up a few feet to my left, lunge at me.

"Mr. Garrick, my name's Dan—"

"So?" he says, cutting me off.

"I've come to ask you a favor."

No response.

"I was walking through the woods the other day, and I ended up on your property."

Still no response.

"I ran into Benji Samuels."

"Was he drunk?"

"Huh, well, huh—"

"Was he?"

"I think he had been drinking, but I don't believe he was drunk."

"What are you? Some damned politician or diplomat?"

"Sir?"

"Benji's always drunk. So you were on my land. You come up here just to tell me you were on my land. You do it again, and next time, I'll shoot you."

"That's what Benji told me," I say with a little laugh.

"Well, good for him—he's right. What are you doing here, anyway?"

"I want to take pictures of your land, and I'd like your permission."

"Go to hell."

"I brought some of my photos with me to show you," I blurt out, ignoring Garrick's last comment. "I'm good. Look," I say, pulling out an eight-by-ten black-and-white photo of some of the ice-covered fir trees by the river.

Slowly Garrick's eyes move toward the photo in my hand. He studies it for a moment and then, like a skittish pup sniffing a stranger's food, Garrick takes the photo from me.

"You got more like this?"

"Yes, sir. Can I show them to you?"

"What did you say your name was?"

"Danny Murtaugh."

Garrick pauses and looks at me. "Charles and Linda's boy?"

"Yes, sir."

He opens the door and swings his head toward the big dining room on the other side of the entranceway. I follow him toward a large table covered with property maps. Off to my right, on a table by the door, I catch the glint of the bluish gray barrel and light brown handle of a revolver.

"It's a .357 Magnum. At a hundred yards, using the red-dot scope on it, I can hit fifty out of a hundred clay pigeons. At fifty yards, I'm perfect for a heart shot on a buck every time," Garrick says without looking back at me. "And, yes, it is loaded."

Then he turns back to me and smiles slightly. "For woodchucks and squirrels," he says. "Let's see what you got."

I spread out the photographs, glancing around as Garrick studies them.

Well, I've made it to the inner sanctuary of Frederick P. Garrick. It looks a lot like other homes, except for all the maps and the old pictures hanging on the walls.

"Why should I give you permission? What's in it for me?"

"I'll give you first pick of the photos that I take."

Garrick looks up and studies me.

"You're wiry . . . like your father. Yes," he says, as if he's convincing himself of something. "You are like him, all right. But that angel face and the blue eyes—those're your mother."

I open my mouth to respond, but nothing comes out.

"Speechless, hey!" He laughs. "Not used to people being direct with you, are you? Well, I don't like to waste time with chitchat and social crap. So I get to the point."

He opens a drawer, takes a piece of paper with his letterhead on it, and scribbles something.

"Here," he says, handing me the paper. "Permission granted. I'll draw up a formal contract and have my lawyer mail it to you for your signature."

"Thanks," I say, though I'm unsure about the lawyer part.

"Now, I got work to do. You got what you wanted. I'd better see some good photographs from you."

"Thanks," I say again, walking past the shiny revolver on the table by the door.

"Your father was a good man," Garrick says suddenly. "He

was honest, and he cared about people."

"Thank you, Mr. Garrick."

"'Thank you' isn't necessary. It's just a fact, that's all."

"Thanks just the same."

six

"Hey, Billy," I holler from the window of the old red pickup, which, along with the thirty-aught-six semiautomatic rifle hanging on the rack, was one of the last remnants of my father in my life. "You got some time? Got somethin' to show you."

"Okay. I'll meet you at the diner," Billy hollers back.

Charlie's Diner was about dead set in the center of town. It was a throwback to the fifties—a converted trailer with the out-of-use railroad tracks rusting behind the back door. People in town call it "Up Chucks," but they still go there for a hamburger, sandwich, and cup of coffee, even though the prices are steep.

Billy got there ahead of me and was already sitting down in one of the green plastic booths in the back room, so I slid into the seat across from him.

"Take a look at this," I say, shoving Garrick's note across the table.

Billy looks at the letterhead and studies the writing for a minute. "Impressive. Though you can barely read the old man's handwriting."

"Just came from his house."

"Still have his maps spread out all over?"

"Yeah, how'd you know?"

"Been that way for years. First time I was in his house, I was eleven years old. I was with your dad and Benji.

"The three of us spent a summer together, just hunting and fishing. One of the best times I ever had. Benji and your dad were about fourteen, I think. One day we got caught by Old Man Garrick trout fishing in his river. It was a warm day in March, before the season was open, so we were breaking the law. But that wasn't what got Garrick mad."

"You were on his land, right?"

"Yeah, but we were with Benji. And Benji always had permission. His dad was caretaker for Garrick. And I think Garrick had, maybe even still does have, a soft spot for kids. Especially for Benji. Anyway, that wasn't why he was mad. It was because we were fishing with worms, and no gentleman ever fished for trout using worms. It was flies—wet or dry—but flies, or it was nothing."

"What'd he do?"

"He marched us into his house to show us his fly collection, explain why we should use flies, and then gave us permission to fish, but only if we used flies."

"So did you?"

"Not always, but we made damn sure we always had a fly-fishing rod ready to go just in case he showed up."

"Coffee?"

I look up into the green eyes behind the voice. Soft, creamy-smooth face, long auburn hair partially pulled back so that her curls fall down across her shoulders.

"Coffee?" she repeats.

"Just coffee for me," says Billy. "Did you eat yet?"

"Uh, me, yes. I mean, no. No, I didn't. But, yeah, what are you havin'? Anything?"

"Just coffee. You want somethin' to eat?" says Billy.

"No, no, that's fine. Nothin'."

"Nothin'?" says the waitress.

"Well, maybe."

"Maybe?" she says.

"Maybe, coffee?"

"Coffee?" she says.

"Okay, coffee."

"Two coffees," she says.

"Fine," says Billy to her, then smirks at me as she heads into the kitchen. "Heck of a first impression, kid."

"That bad, huh?"

"Well, except for the stuttering, your jaw on the table, your tongue hangin' out, and the spit drooling down your chin, I'd say you made a very good impression."

"Who is she?"

"Dunno. First time I've seen her," says Billy. "So you got permission from Garrick, huh?"

"Yeah. He didn't seem that bad—except maybe for the revolver on the table by the door."

"What did he want in return?"

"What?"

"He doesn't ever do anything for free. Whad'ja agree to?"

"I told him I'd give him some photographs," I say.

"He draw up a contract?"

"No—but he did say his lawyer would. I figured he was kidding."

"He never kids. You'll get the contract in a couple of days. Hey, Charlie, " Billy calls to the diner owner.

"Billy, how are ya? Haven't seen you in here in a while," says

Charlie as he walks over to the booth. "Hey, Danny. Good to see you, too. How's your mom?"

"She's doing fine."

"Tell her I said hello."

"Will do."

"Say, Charlie, who's the new girl workin' for you?"

"Oh, Stephanie? She started workin' here 'bout a week ago. Hard worker, that much I know. She's a niece of Ruthie Garrell. Seems like a nice kid. Why, you know somebody who's interested?" he says, smiling at me.

"Charlie, you got people wantin' to pay," one of the waitresses yells out.

"Gotta go. Money waitin' to be taken."

"Thanks," I say to Billy sheepishly.

"Over to you now."

"Right, just what I need—another opportunity for rejection."

"Well, you gotta get over old what's-her-name sooner or later. You can't go through your life whining and moaning because you got cheated on. Happens to lots of people."

"Happen to you?"

Billy looks at me. "Maybe," he says. "Yeah, s'pose it did. Long time ago."

"Whad'ya do?"

"At the time, nothin'. Took a while, but I got over it. Listen, you got a life ahead of you. A great life. You have magic in those fingers. They didn't give you a full ride to music college because you were average. You're a piano player. You gotta get over this."

"Mom tell you to tell me this?"

"Danny, I'm not gonna lie to you. Of course, she told me

to tell you. But I believe it, too. Forget the girl. Let it go. Get on with your life."

"I know, I know. But it's gonna take some time. You know, I don't even think it's about her anymore. I don't know. I just don't know what I want to do. So I guess I'll just take pictures of woods for a while."

"Listen, Danny, you can do what you want, but be careful around Garrick. There's more trouble there than you realize. And don't go tellin' people that you have permission to be on his land. In fact, don't go tellin' anybody that you've been up to his place. The fewer people know about that, the better."

"What are you talkin' about?"

"Just keep quiet about all that, all right?"

"I told you, you're not welcome in here!" Charlie's voice echoes off the old photos of trains hanging haphazardly on the back wall. "Now, get the hell out."

A dark-haired teen slinks toward two guys sitting in a silver Toyota.

"What was that all about?" asks Billy, handing Charlie a twenty.

"Raymond Barnes."

"Who?" asks Billy.

"I know him," I say. "A year younger than me. Lives up near Benji. Got caught dealing drugs a year ago. I thought they put him in jail."

"Yeah, well, he's out," says Charlie. "I know that son of a bitch ripped me off. I could never prove it, but I know it. I'll be damned if I ever let him use my pay phone."

The silver Toyota heads away with a lone finger saluting good-bye.

"Same to you, you little creep," says Charlie.

seven

"Hey! I thought I told you to stay off Mr. Garrick's land!"

"I got permission!" I yell to Benji Samuels across a field of pale green tufts of early spring grass. His red-and-black flannel shirt is muted against the forest line of big firs, marking the edge of Frederick P. Garrick's property.

"Humph!" he scoffs as he walks toward me, rifle hanging loosely at his side. "Let's see it."

I pull out the paper and slosh through the muddy field to meet Benji.

He grabs it out of my hand, then holds it up in the sunlight and squints.

"How do I know you didn't forge this?"

"I guess you don't."

Benji looks at me. "Don't s'pose Chuck Murtaugh's son would lie," he says finally. "Anyways, I'd find out sooner or later."

"S'pose so."

"Well, this calls for a celebration," he says suddenly, pulling out a silver flask. "Here, have a snort."

"No, thanks."

"What? Too good to drink with Benji Samuels?"

"No, no," I say quickly, not wanting to upset a man who has a rifle in his hand. "It's just that I don't drink much."

"Your old man wasn't too good to drink with me."

Benji's words sting. There's so much about my dad I don't know. Won't ever know.

"Him and me tied a few good ones on, that's for sure."

The sting goes deeper. It turns into pain. That's the way it is. Sometimes nothing, and then, out of nowhere, there it is.

"Yes, sir, fishin' all day, a few brewskis at night. Your old man, he was somethin'."

"I guess I never saw my father drink much," I say mechanically.

Benji looks at my blank face.

"Tell ya what," says Benji, "come on back to my place. I got somethin' to show you."

"What?"

"Never you mind, boy. You just do what Benji tells you."

"I can't. I got pictures to take."

"You'll have time for pictures. First you won't drink with Benji, now you're too good to come to his house when he invites you?"

"No, it's just that—"

"Come on, then," he says, wrapping his strong arm around my neck. "Gonna be worth your while, boy."

I stiffen. Then I straighten my back up and pull away from him.

Quickly Benji lets go and steps away. He tilts his head to one side and squints.

What does he see standing here in front of him? A kid? All one hundred seventy pounds hung on a six-foot bony frame. Curly blond hair, cut short, my blue eyes set deep in my mother's "angel" face. But I've got an anger inside of me that he doesn't know.

And what about Benji? Two inches shorter, wiry like me, but hard and muscular, no fat on him. His face red from drinking, black eyes surrounded by the haze of cigarettes and booze, his body swaying slightly side to side.

We could be at each other in a flash.

"Sorry," I mumble. "I don't like people doin' that."

"Just got a few pictures of your dad I wanted to show you. That's all," says Benji, sulking.

"I'm sorry," I say again. "I'd like to see the pictures."

Benji shakes his head. "Don't do me any favors."

"No, I mean it. I'd really like to see them."

Benji jerks his head toward a path through the deep evergreens, and I follow in silence.

"You been here all your life?" I say. What a stupid thing to say. Of course, he's been here all his life. He was born here, and he'll die here.

"Yeah."

Silence.

"How long did you know my father?"

"Long time."

More silence.

"I know he was a good fisherman."

"The best."

"Better than you?" I ask.

Benji stops suddenly and looks at me.

"Nobody's better than me."

"Nobody?" I say with a smile.

"Nobody," he says seriously.

Stillness in the forest. Down a winding path covered in pine needles stands a large log house, wraparound porch on three sides—torn shades hanging in the windows, screen door off its hinges, old Jeep rusting in the grass-covered driveway, pink refrigerator resting comfortably on its side nearby.

"Home," says Benji matter-of-factly.

"It's . . . big," I say, trying to find some kind of compliment.

"Humph," says Benji.

We walk up the steps.

I follow him inside. A glass cabinet, framed in dark wood and stacked meticulously with rifles and handguns, stands sentinel amid piles of newspapers, magazines, empty beer cans, and dirty dishes everywhere. How does a person end up like this?

A cat rises from its rest on the kitchen counter and purrs, hoping for some stroke of attention from me, the stranger in the house.

Benji goes over to the refrigerator and pulls out a can of beer.

"Here," he says, handing it to me. "And don't give me any crap about not drinkin'. You are in the home of Benji Samuels, and by God, you're gonna have a drink with him."

I pop the lid on the can.

"Here's to your father," he says, and swallows a gulp from his flask.

I hold up the can and nod slightly.

"That's more like it," Benji says. He studies me. "Yeah, you and me could go at it, but don't you think for a moment you could whip me. I'd kick your ass."

I stare back. "Maybe. Maybe not."

Benji doesn't say anything. I know he's struggling with whether to fight me because of what I just said. I know he thinks it's an insult in his own house.

"Wouldn't be right," he says finally.

Benji walks into the living room, opens a drawer, and pulls out some photos. "Bet ya ain't seen these."

And he was right. I had never seen these photos. There was my father, just a few years younger than I am now, sitting on Benji's porch, holding up a beer. And there he was fishing down in the river just fifty yards from Benji's house. And there, holding up a big trout, chest puffed out in half-serious gloating. And there with one arm around Benji, another around a younger boy.

"Who's that?" I ask, touching the boy in the photo.

"Humph! That is Billy—state gestapo—Taylor."

I pause, nod my head slowly, but I don't look at Benji.

I thought the boy in the photo was Billy, but I don't say so. In the world of Benji Samuels and Frederick P. Garrick, anyone who works for the state is evil. I don't see evil in Billy, and I don't see evil in Benji or in Frederick P. Garrick.

"Who took the picture?"

"What?"

"The picture with the three of you in it. Who took it? Garrick?"

"Garrick? No, the old man's kid brother, Ryan."

"Here, have another beer," says Benji. "Best summer I ever had. We was fourteen, your dad and me. Our birthdays were only a week apart. Billy, he maybe just turned twelve. Back then, he idolized your father, you know."

I nod again. I had heard that.

"That trout there that your father's holdin'. That's the biggest rainbow I ever seen taken from this river. He was usin' a black-and-white bucktail." Benji studies the photo, looking for the clues that will bring him back in time. He looks up at me—like I'm one of the clues. "Have another beer, kid," he says.

"No, I'm fine," I say, holding up my half-full can.

"Come on, boy, you gotta catch up with me," says Benji. He looks back at the photo. "Day your dad caught that big rainbow, he told us to use Leadwing Coachman. Then the son of a bitch lands this huge fish. When he pulls the fly out, I get a look at it. 'Leadwing Coachman,' I says to him when I see the black-and-white bucktail hangin' from that trout's mouth. He just smiles at me. 'Luck,' he says. Yes, sir, your dad was somethin'. He was the best."

"Fisherman?" slips the word from my lips.

Benji squints hard and stares right into my eyes.

"I'm the best," he says, then he pauses. "Your dad was the best." He takes another drink from the silver flask.

"I gotta get goin', Benji."

He nods.

"These are great pictures. Thanks for showing them to me."

"I should give 'em to you," he says suddenly. "But I can't."

"They're yours."

"I know, but he was your father."

"He was your friend."

"When I die, kid, you come an' get 'em."

"Thanks."

"I mean it."

"I know."

eight

"You've been drinking."

I wish we had a bigger kitchen!

"I had a beer," I say, trying to pretend like this is an everyday occurrence, which it is not.

"Correct me if I'm wrong, but the legal drinking age in this state is twenty-one, correct?"

I roll my eyes.

"I thought you said you were going to take pictures."

"I did."

"So how did you end up getting drunk?"

"I'm not drunk. I had a beer."

"I asked you a question: How did you end up—Jesus Christ! You weren't up there drinkin' with Benji Samuels, were you? For God's sake! I can't believe it. My son drinking with that old bum!"

"He's not an old bum!"

"Then what is he? He has no job. He lives in a shack. He's drunk almost all the time. If that isn't a bum, I don't know what is."

"He doesn't live in a shack."

Now she rolls her eyes.

"He showed me some pictures he had of Dad."

That stops her dead.

"When they were kids—Dad and him and Billy."

Her mouth closes and her lips tighten.

"They were good friends."

"You can't be spending your days drinking with Benji Samuels," she says, quietly returning to her original point.

"I'm not spending my days drinking with Benji," I say.

"You did today. Danny, it's been almost four months since you left college. You can't just drift along doing nothing. You need to figure out what you're going to do. And you need to do that now."

"I'm paying you rent."

"This isn't about paying rent, but since you bring it up, you're paying me with money that your grandfather had set aside for college. You need to be back in college, but until you do go back, you need to get a job, and I mean it."

"Okay, okay."

"I'm serious, Danny. I mean now."

A car door slams and Jasper yelps.

"Anybody home?" Billy calls from the front porch.

"What's going to happen to you? I swear to God, you had everything going for you and here you are falling apart in front of me."

"I'm not falling apart."

She turns her head. "In the kitchen," she calls back to Billy.

"Hey, how's everybody to— Want me to come back later?"

"He was drinking all day with Benji Samuels."

"Oh. Maybe I'll come back later."

"Maybe you can talk some sense into him. He won't listen to me."

Billy looks at her, then at me.

"He showed me some pictures of my dad," I say, finally.

Mom grunts and turns back to cutting her carrots.

Billy smiles.

"Really?" he says.

"You were in one."

"Yeah, I know the picture you mean. I haven't seen it in years."

"Hey, I didn't know Garrick had a brother."

The carrot cutting stops. Billy looks up at Mom.

"What? What'd I say?"

"Some brother," she says. "A spoiled rich kid."

"You knew him?"

"Not really," she says. "He would come around sometimes in the summer."

"Benji show you the picture of your father with that trout?" asks Billy, changing the subject.

"Yeah. Quite a fish."

Billy and I slide softly into a conversation about fishing and Benji and Dad, and Mom, at the edge of the talk, with sharp knife in hand, clicks the carrots quickly.

nine

Barely Bach, I think to myself as piano notes from the Harpsichord Concerto no. 5 in F Minor come from one of the practice rooms at the community college. Could be worse. At least it's recognizable.

I tack up another ad on a community bulletin board in the music hall:

PIANO LESSONS FOR ALL AGES
Just getting started? Wanting to restart?
Have a talented youngster? Or oldster?
Give me a call: 845-555-0749.
References on request.

Well, this is one way to make a few bucks until I decide what to do with my life. At least I can tell her that I'm doing something to try to earn some money, which oughta get her off my back.

Bach's Concerto gets choppier. The perfectionist in me has to know, so I wander over to the open door of one of the music rooms. I've got to see who's butchering Bach, I think, peering into the room.

The waitress from the diner looks up.

"Sorry," I say and start to leave, but the moment seizes me. *What've you got to lose?* "My name's Danny Murtaugh." I hold out my hand.

She looks at my hand and then up at my face.

"Stephanie," she says, slowly reaching up to my outstretched hand.

"Could I make a suggestion?" I say.

She looks up at me, arching her eyebrows skeptically.

"You're playing it a little too abruptly."

"Really," she says, her voice flat. "I suppose you'd like to show me how you think it is supposed to be played."

"May I?"

She stands up and says, "It's all yours, maestro."

I sit down at the piano. "It's been a while since I played."

She doesn't say anything.

I raise my hands gently above the keys. It has been four months since I've played. I tried to tell myself that I would never play again, but really I only needed a reason to start. And here she was, green eyes staring at me to see if I can deliver. I look at the dots on the page of the music and smile. My fingers begin the dance, and the dots blur. . . .

I raise my hands from the keys as the last note fades.

Stephanie stares. "That was incredible! You are good!"

"Thanks, but it's Bach who's good."

"How long have you been playing?"

"Oh, since I was a little kid."

"Are you going to school now? A conservatory or something?"

"I was."

"What do you mean 'was'?"

"It's a long story."

"They always are."

"What?"

"Whenever it involves a girl, it's a long story."

"What?"

She shakes her head and chuckles. "Long stories are always about girls—or guys," she says, smiling.

I'm not going to blow this chance.

"Can I buy you a cup of coffee?"

The smile disappears.

ten

"The cafeteria's right downstairs, or we could go to the diner in town, if that's better?" I say, trying to draw her back from wherever she's gone.

She says nothing.

"I'm sorry. I didn't mean to upset you."

"No, no. You didn't . . . I mean, it's just that . . . well, it's a long story."

"A guy?"

"No, not really, well, yes, kind of . . . It is a long story."

"Well, I promise to give you my shortened version, and you can give me your shortened version—or the long version," I say. "Or no version at all," I add, hoping not to lose the moment.

She smiles. "Okay. Coffee, downstairs."

"Good. So, there was a girl," I say, starting my story as we walk downstairs.

"What was her name?"

"Kaitlyn. With a K. Want a cappuccino?"

"Sure."

"Two cappuccinos," I say to the girl behind the coffee counter.

"So what happened with Kaitlyn?"

"Found her with another guy."

"What did you do?"

"Nothing. Just stood there."

"She didn't say anything?"

"She smiled. Where do you wanna sit?" I say, picking up two mugs of cappuccino.

"Over by the door, so either of us can make a fast exit if we need to."

"It won't be me," I say.

"Don't bet on it. So what then?"

"Well, I disintegrated. I couldn't go to classes. I stopped playing the piano. And a couple of weeks after it happened, I quit school."

Stephanie sips the cappuccino and looks at me. "So you quit school, and every time you think of Kaitlyn with a K you see her with some guy."

"Kinda pathetic, isn't it?"

"Yeah, it is."

"You didn't have to agree."

"It is."

"Like I said, 'You don't have to agree.'"

"You wanna leave?"

"No. So that's my shortened version of the long story. What about you?"

"You know, it's a funny thing about quitting: it's just because we're mad."

"What do you mean?"

"Quitting. It's just because we can't stand the way it's all turned out. Some people punch holes in the wall. Some shut down. Or take drugs. Or kill themselves. Or quit school. Any way you look at it, it's quitting."

"Maybe. Never thought about it like that."

"But you did quit."

"Yeah, well, I was asking about you."

Slowly she rubs the mug up and down with both her hands.

"You always do that when you get nervous?"

"What?"

"That," I say, looking at the mug.

"Oh, that."

"Yeah, that. Wanna leave?"

"No."

"So, back to your story."

"Well . . ."

"Yes?"

"Well, the real short version is I'm taking some classes here at the community college, trying to get started on a BA in English and—I have a three-year-old daughter."

The pause hangs in the air, and I mumble, "Oh."

"Yeah, that always gets a guy's attention," she says. "Now you're ready to leave?"

"No."

Longer pause.

"That's it?" I ask. "Isn't there more?"

"Not to the short version."

"And the long version?"

"I really can't go into it now."

"Okay, when?"

Suddenly she sits up straight, her hands drop away from the cup, and she looks directly at me. "I've got to go."

"Okay," I say. "Can I have your phone number?"

She shakes her head. "Give me yours."

I write it on a napkin and give it to her.

"Okay, I'll call you—or maybe I won't."

"So, I wait for you to call me—or not?"

"That's it. You wait."

"Why can't I call you?"

"I have my reasons."

"You know, this doesn't seem quite fair."

"Is it supposed to be?"

"Well—"

"Should we ask Kaitlyn with a K?"

"You have a point. Wait, huh?"

"That's it. Just wait. Now I do have to leave," she says, standing up. "Three-year-olds don't wait."

eleven

Bam! A single shot cracks the air.

I hop from my truck and walk nervously toward the front door. The big dogs in their pen lunge at me.

"You lookin' for me, boy?" comes Frederick P. Garrick's voice from the far corner of a garden just beyond the house. "Got 'em," he says, holding up the limp body of a woodchuck. "At forty yards, too. Come on in," he says, entering the house, woodchuck dangling from one hand, pistol in the other. "They're not much for eatin'," he says, holding up the dead animal, "but I chop them up and freeze them for dog food. The dogs get a taste of them and then they go after them on their own. So, you got some pictures for me?"

"Yes, sir."

"Good. Let's take a look," he says, eyeing the bag I'm holding.

"What the hell is this?" he says, pointing at the packages of photos I pull out. "I don't have time to go through all of these. I want them in binders so that I can look at them without having to sort through all this," he says. "Didn't you get my contract?"

"Yes, sir, but I—"

"I spelled out exactly what I want in the contract."

"Sorry—"

"Did you even read the contract?"

"Well, I—"

"You didn't, did you?"

"Well—"

"Did you sign it? Because if you signed it without reading it, you are an idiot, and I won't work with people who are idiots. I'm tired of working with idiots. The whole goddamned world is made up of idiots. Those asses who work for the state are idiots. Even my own lawyers are idiots. I hope the hell you aren't one, too."

"I didn't sign the contract."

"Good. But you haven't read it, either, have you?"

"No, sir."

"So, you're a moron, not an idiot. But at least you're an honest moron."

"Thanks, I think."

"Just show me the pictures that are the best. Next time have them in a binder for me."

"Yes, sir."

I pull out some of the photos. "I've got a few I think you'll like."

"Pretty good for an amateur," he says, looking at them.

I just shoot what I like, I think.

Garrick pauses on one photo. "You found the overlook."

I nod.

"It's the only place where you can see clearly how my river goes into the big river. Get me an eight-by-ten of this one."

"Sure."

He stares at the picture. "I was standing there when it happened."

I take a deep breath, because I know what Garrick is about

to say.

"I don't s'pose you knew that."

"No, sir."

"I wanted to see how bad the runoff was from all the rain we had had. I got up to the overlook, right where you took this. I looked out at my muddy river, and then I saw the dog in the middle of it, bobbing toward the big river. I knew it was my dog. Roman was his name. He was just barely a year old and had gone off chasing a deer the day before. I looked across, and there you and your father were, standing on the opposite shore. You know, as soon as I saw you two, I knew he would do it. I thought to myself, 'Charles, don't do it. It's just a dog.' But I knew he would. I saw it all. I stood right there and watched. There wasn't a god-damned thing I could do.

"Nothing I could do but watch."

twelve

"He was probably more interested in the dog."

You're wrong about him!

My mother leans closer to the mirror and coats her lips with pale pink lipstick.

"Yeah, it was his dog in that river," she says as we get into the truck on our way to town to meet Billy for lunch. "Get in the back, Jasper." She pauses before she slides onto the seat and stares blankly at me. "His stupid dog in the river."

I grip the steering wheel a little tighter; my foot presses on the gas a little more firmly. My mother stares out the window at the passing chartreuse buds of forsythia on the verge of bloom. Jasper stands in the back of the pickup, sniffing the cold spring air as hints of worlds beyond his own blow quickly by him. On we ride. Not one more word spoken until we pull into the parking lot of the diner.

"We never talk about it," I say, turning off the key.

"What?"

"His death."

"I know."

"Should we?"

"Probably."

"But not today," I say.

"No, not today. C'mon, Jasper," she says to the big dog. "Hop in the front." She turns back to me and touches me lightly on the arm. "Billy's waitin' inside."

So we walk away again from some conversation we both think we should have into the diner toward Billy. Stephanie rushes by, a plate of burgers and fries balancing on her fingertips.

"Hi," she says.

"Hi."

"Still waiting?" she says.

"Patiently."

"I doubt you're patient."

"I'm learning."

"What was that all about?" my mother asks.

"Girl I met. Been here long?" I say to Billy as I sit down across from him.

"No. Couple of minutes."

I glance at my mother as she sits down next to Billy. Ah, Mom, I know what you're thinking: another girl, just what he needs. He can't get over the last one, and here comes another one.

A man in a red-checkered flannel shirt, staggering across the street, interrupts my thoughts.

"Is that Benji Samuels?" I say out loud.

"Yeah, I guess so," says Billy, turning toward the window.

"Drunk as usual," says my mother.

"You don't know that," I say defensively.

"Really? Sure looks it to me," she says, nodding her head toward Benji, who bobs and stumbles across the street, stopping cars as he goes. Slowly he works his way toward the red pickup truck.

"Oh, jeez," my mother says with a sigh.

Benji Samuels finds his way to our pickup and pets the wet

nose of Jasper sticking out of the partially open window. Benji looks around, sees us through the diner window, and heads toward us.

"I better go outside," says Billy, heading quickly to meet Benji before he gets in the diner.

"I'll go with you," I say, hopping up.

"I think I'll just wait right here," says Mom, settling in behind the menu in front of her face.

"Benji," says Billy on the outside steps. "How are you? Long time, no see."

"Humph!" says Benji.

"Hello, Benji," I say.

"What you doin' wi' him?" Benji says to me.

"Well, we were just about to have lunch."

"What you eatin' lunch wi' that somabitch for?"

"Benji, come on . . ." coaxes Billy.

"Don't you talk to me. I got notin' to say to you," he says to Billy and then turns to me. "You shudn' be wi' him. He's no good. No good. He's—" Benji stops and looks behind me.

"Hello, Benji."

I turn to see my mother standing in the doorway of the diner.

Benji nods his head politely. "Linda."

"It's been a long time."

"Yesssh, it has. He shudn' be wi' him," he says suddenly, turning back to me. "His dad wudin' like it."

"Billy and Chuck were friends, Benji. You know that."

"Nah! He doesn't know wat it means to be a friend," says Benji, and then he spits at Billy's feet.

"You're lucky you're drunk," says Billy coldly.

"Drunk! Who's drunk? C'mon. We'll go at it right here. Ah kick ya ass, right here! Right now. I'm not too drunk for that."

"Benji, whaddaya doin'?" comes a voice from behind him.

Benji freezes.

"Come on, Benji," says a stocky woman with short, wavy, gray and black hair, cigarette hanging loosely from her mouth. She slips her hand under Benji's arm and quickly wraps her arm around it, clamping it tight with her other hand.

"Come on, Benji. It's me, Ruthie Garrell. Why don't we take a walk?"

"These people, theez people—" he starts, but Ruthie cuts him off.

"Ah, these people, these people, the hell with these people," she says, winking at me and throwing her cigarette to the ground. "Let's you and me go for a walk. Come on," she says again to him more strongly.

Benji hesitates, starts to stiffen and pull away.

Just like out in the woods! I think. Just like it was between me and him. He's gonna go after Billy unless—

"Okay if I join you?" I say suddenly.

Benji looks at me and softens. "Okay," he says quietly.

Billy starts to say something, but a quick, hard look from Ruthie stops him.

"This could take a while, Mom. Can Billy take you home?"

"Sure," she says quietly.

t h i r t e e n

"Benji, Benji, Benji, what are we gonna do with you?" says Ruthie, her hands still wrapped strongly around his arm, as she tugs him down the sidewalk.

Benji turns his stare from Billy and looks at her.

"I'm just no good, Ruthie. No good." The words drip from his lips.

"Why'd you stop goin' to meetings?"

"I couldn't get no rides."

"That's not true, Benji, and you know it. All you had to do was call, and someone would have come and gotten you."

"I din' wanna be callin' people all the time."

"I've told you this before, Benji, anytime you need a ride, I'll come and get you. If it wasn't for you, I'd a never gotten sober. You were the one I listened to at all those early meetings. I was such a mess, and most of the others had all those years of sobriety, but you, you were right out of it, just fresh off the booze, just like me. If you weren't there, I wouldn'a made it."

Benji says nothing, but hangs his head.

"Why don't you come to a meeting tonight?"

"Don't have no ride."

"I'll come an' get you. Meeting's at eight; I'll pick you up at quarter after seven. Okay?"

Benji doesn't answer.

"Okay, Benji. I'll be there at seven fifteen. You need a ride home now?"

Again, Benji says nothing.

"Well, how'd you get into town?"

"I was walkin' an summin' picked me up," he says.

"So you don't have a ride home. Well, let's see what we can do. I've gotta pick up my niece as soon as she's done working. I suppose I could bring you along, drop her off, and then take you home."

"Don' wan' no ride," says Benji.

"I can give him a ride," I say.

Ruthie looks quickly at me. "It would be a big help, if you could," she says. "But he's a handful when he's drinking. You gonna behave yourself, Benji?"

"I can walk," he says, staring at the ground. "Don' nee' no ride."

"Don't let him drink anymore."

"How do I stop him?"

Ruthie pauses and looks at me, then she turns to Benji. "Benji, you listen to me. Put the booze away for the rest of the day."

"You know I can't do that, Ruthie."

"You can do it just for the rest of the day."

Benji doesn't answer.

"You wanna get sober?"

Benji doesn't answer.

"I'm comin' over to get you tonight, whether you want me to or not. I owe you that, Benjamin Samuels. You better not be drunk. Okay?"

Benji doesn't answer.

"Okay?"

"Okay," he mutters as they turn the corner of the block near my truck.

I open the door, and Ruthie pours Benji into the cab next to Jasper.

"Try to not let him drink too much, anyway," says Ruthie as I hop into the driver's seat, and then she adds, "You know she has a three-year-old daughter?"

"What?" I say.

"My niece, Stephanie. You know she has a daughter."

"Yes. She told me."

"She's just getting back on her feet. She doesn't need to get involved with a guy."

"There's no involvement."

"Just the same, she doesn't need to get involved."

I look out the windshield, straight ahead, and turn the key.

"Maybe I don't need to get involved, either," I say defensively.

"Good. Don't," she says, pulling out another cigarette.

I blink a couple of times, grind the gear on the old truck into first, and pull away, with Ruthie Garrell standing in the street, pulling a long breath on her cigarette.

Just out of second gear, Benji pulls out his silver flask.

"Hey, Benji, you told Ruthie you wouldn't drink."

Benji doesn't answer.

"Benji, you're not supposed to be drinking."

"I'll drink when I wanna. Nobody's gonna tell me when I drink."

"She's going to take you to some meeting tonight."

"Maybe I don' wanna go."

"You told her you would."

"She oughta min' her own business."

"She's gonna come and get you tonight."

"So?"

"So, you said you'd be sober."

"Did not."

I shake my head. There's no use arguing with a drunk. For one thing, I wouldn't win, and besides, I think he's right—I don't think he did say he'd be sober.

The old truck rattles into third gear, cars honking, drivers sticking their heads out behind me and edging past on a long hill. By fourth gear, a silver Toyota with the three guys who were at the diner the other day speeds by, still stuck in single-finger salute, while Benji Samuels sips slowly from his shiny flask. I rechew my sweet anger with Ruthie Garrell and her warning to stay away from her niece—who may, or may not, call me.

fourteen

By the time we arrive at his house, Benji is half-asleep, mumbling every so often about Frederick Garrick, Billy Taylor, the land, the river, and his only true friend, Chuck Murtaugh.

"Benji, we're home."

"Humph. What? Home? Where's home? What home?"

"Your home, Benji. Come on. I'll help you."

"Ge' away fra me!" he yells, pushing me back. "I don' nee' no hel'. No hel'. No, sir. No. No hel'. Bennnnji Samu' don' nee' hel' from no one."

"Suit yourself. Just don't fall on your face," I say, walking close behind him as he staggers up his porch.

"Nee' a drink. That's wha' I nee'. A drink."

"Benji, don't you think you've had enough?" I say, following him into the house.

"A drin', thass wha' I nee," he says, picking up a half-full bottle of Jack Daniels and a glass.

"Come on, Benji. Why don't you lie down for a while," I say, trying to slide the bottle away from him.

"You get your goddamn hands off my drin'!" Benji shouts, pushing me away. "Who the hell you thin' you are, comin' in the house of Benji Samu' and tellin' him he can' drink! You get outta here!"

"Okay. Okay. Take it easy."

"You get outta here. No one tells Benji Samu' he can' drink. No one!" he screams, flinging his arm across the littered kitchen counter, sending greasy plates and glasses smashing into the wall.

Benji pauses and looks at me. He walks slowly, like a paralyzed man getting back his walk—one step toward me, a stutter, two steps, closer, a stumble, steady himself on the counter. So close now that the sweet smell of the silver-flasked booze, steeping in the sour spit of his mouth and seeping through the acrid sweat of his body, rises into my nose and swims inside my own mouth, gagging me, as I hold down vomit.

"No one can tell me I can' drink. No one can tell me wha' ta do. An' I'll tell you why," Benji whispers. "I go' Fred Pissy Garrick and the grea' state park rangers by the royal balls," he says suddenly, sweeping his right hand from the air down. "By the fuckin' balls," he says with a smile, squeezing his hand tight in a powerful gesture.

"They think I'm a retar'. They thin' I don' know nothin'. But I know. I know Mr. Bigshot up there in his fancy house can' do nothin' withou' me. I got a li' piece of paper, signed by old Pisshead's granddad himself, the granddad of all the pisshead Garricks, an' signed by my granddad, too, sayin' he can' sell this land unless I give my permission, which I ain't gonna. So, old Mr. P. Garrick, he'll just hav'ta keep payin' me, like he paid my father, an' his father before him. Keep payin' me, cause I got 'im by the balls.

"An' you know som'in', you know, 'cuz you are Charles Winston Murtaugh's good son, an' becuz' he was the only fren' I ever had, I mean, the only fren." Benji pauses, and tears start to come. I cringe. "The only one who like' me for me," he says, pounding himself on the chest. "For me, for who I was. Because you are his son, I will show you som'in' only one other person seen, an' that was him, your father, and he's dead, an' there waddin' nofin I coul' do 'bout it. He died in that goddamn river! Tryin' to save some somabitchin' dog! A dog! A somabitchin' dog! An' they call me a retar'! I ain't so stupid to go after some somabitchin' dog in the river in a flood. I'm no' goin' do that. No, I couldn' do that. Why did you do that, Chuck? Why?" He collapses in a chair, weeping. "You were my only fren'. Only one, an' you died tryin' to save a dog. You know he di' that? Try to save a dog?" he says, looking at me.

"Yes, Benji, I know. I was there."

Then Benji straightens up in his chair and looks right at me. The clouds of Jack Daniels seem to clear away and he asks, "Why did he do that, Danny?"

"I don't know, " I say instinctively, because I've said it so many times before. But it was a lie. I do know why my father jumped in a flooded river to save a dog. I can still hear my voice crying, "Daddy, Daddy, a dog! There's a dog in the river! Do something, Daddy! You can't let him drown! You can't! Do something!"

And so my father did something. He did what I asked him to do.

From across the room, Benji suddenly asks, "You gonna stay wi' me?"

"What?"

"You stay wi' me."

"Well, yeah, okay, I can stay—for a little while."

"You stay wi' me!"

"Sure, Benji. Sure, I'll stay."

"Okay, okay. You stay. You, you sit. Sit down. Okay. Good."

So I sit in an old, soft chair, looking at Benji—his head back, eyes wide open, hands clenched on his chair.

fifteen

Settling in. Benji's eyes closing. Sleep easing in. Soon I can slip away in the night, to get back home in time for a call from Stephanie, but Jasper's howls break that hope in pieces.

"Wha's that! Wha's goin on!" yells Benji, jumping from his chair.

"It's just my dog, Benji. It's okay. It's okay," I say, guiding him back to his chair. "Let me go see what's going on. I'll be right back.

"Jasper! What the hell are you doin'?"

More barking from the edge of the woods.

"Jasper! Come on, boy!"

Jasper turns his big golden head back toward my call, kind of smiles, wags his tail, and trots back.

"You'd bark at a leaf, wouldn't you?"

The old dog bounds up the steps, and I dutifully scratch him behind the ear.

"Who's got who trained?" I say to him.

The toilet flushes as I open the screen door to the house, and out comes Benji, a large manila envelope in one hand, a blue steel revolver in the other.

"I told you I got proof," he says. "Take a look," he says, handing me the envelope. "Go ahead, open it."

I just stare at the pistol in Benji's hand.

"Go on," he says, motioning with the gun. "Look."

I look down at the document, handwritten in big swirling script.

"All there. Frederick Pisshead Garrick can't do noth' wit' out me sayin' he can. I got 'im. Only oth' man to see tha' was your father, an' now he's dead," he says, waving the gun in the air. Then he stares hard at me. "You eve' thin' about dyin'?" he says, sitting back down in his chair, resting the gun in his lap.

"Not much."

"I do. Goin' happen."

I nod slightly as I sit in the big, soft chair across from him.

"I think about it," Benji says, taking another drink. "All the time, I thin' 'bout it."

"Benji, don't you think you've had enough?"

"Don't start wit me. Don' you star', " he says, waving the gun again. "I drin' whenev' I wan'. Sooo, don', don' you say nothin'. Okay?"

"Yeah, okay."

"I know wha' I'm doin'," he says, pointing the gun directly at me.

"Benji—"

In a moment I could be dead!

"Benji!"

"Wha? Wha?" he says, looking around, oblivious to what he just did.

"Benji, put the gun away."

"Wha?" he says as he rests the gun on his lap.

Slowly he drifts off. He snores and stops and catches his breath and wakes and curses and jerks and twitches and sleeps.

I lean forward, elbows on my knees, studying him, only seven feet away. Slowly I rise and walk toward the drunken man with the gun.

Quietly, carefully, rhythmically to the sound of Benji's breathing, I reach down toward the gun.

"Awrarfff! Awrarfff!" Jasper's howls rip through silence, snapping Benji back into the moment where all he sees is a man standing over him and, in his drunken dreams, about to kill him.

"Wha! Wha! Wha!" he yells, jumping to his feet.

"Benji! It's just me, Danny. Danny Murtaugh."

But the message doesn't register.

"Wha's goin' on?" he yells, swinging the pistol wildly in the air. The tip of it streaks across my forehead. The feel of something real against something real forces Benji back, and he points the gun directly at the solid thing in front of him—me.

Moments . . .

The taste of blood dripping from my forehead.

On moments . . .

Staring at the things in front of me.

On moments . . .

"Benji," I say softly. "Benji, it's me, Danny Murtaugh. Chuck Murtaugh's son, Danny."

Benji blinks.

The thing in front of him has sound. The sound is a voice. Sweet, nice, safe. Slowly the gun drops to his side, and he sits back in his chair, staring at me, saying nothing.

I dab my hand on my forehead. It's smeared with wet red blood. Lots of it.

"I need to wash my face," I say to Benji. Cautiously, I go to the kitchen sink and find some paper towels to wash the cut.

Benji's eyes follow me all the while. But there is nothing behind his stare, nothing that can connect with who I am and what I'm doing, why I'm here or what just happened.

I look at the clock: four twenty. Three hours till Ruthie shows up.

Paper towels over my forehead, I sit and watch Benji Samuels, who almost killed me, stare.

sixteen

Silence.

Time.

Silence and time.

For two and a half hours.

A car door. Jasper's quick bark.

The scratch of his scrambling paws on the wood floor of the porch outside.

"Benji!"

"In here," I yell.

"Benji," shouts Ruthie, coming in the door, "are you . . . ? " Her voice trails off as she sees him in the chair with the gun and me with blood-soaked paper towels on my head. "My God, what happened?"

"A little accident," I say.

"Did he shoot you?"

"No. Caught me with the gun barrel when I tried to take it from him."

"Benji," she says softly, leaning over him.

The words bring him back. He tilts his head like a puppy hearing a dog barking from the television.

In comes a man, an older woman, and—Stephanie.

"Are you okay?" she asks, coming over to me.

"Yeah."

"Loaded?" the man asks Ruthie as she takes the gun from Benji.

"Yeah, and the gun is, too," she says with a slight laugh.

"Well, looks like we're going to be late for the meeting," says the older woman, looking around. "What a mess."

"Come on, Benji," says the man, leading Benji like a little boy heading to a Sunday night bath. "Let's get you to bed."

"I didn't know what to do when he got the gun," I say to Ruthie.

She shakes her head. "Benji is crazy when he drinks. Crazy. I shouldn't have let you drive him home."

"I thought he might shoot me."

"He might have." She pauses and looks at me. "Why'd you stay?"

"Dunno. Maybe because he was a friend of my dad's."

"Maybe," says Ruthie. "It's what your dad would'a done."

"Where do we start?" says the older woman, looking around the room.

Ruthie sighs and looks at her. "I suppose you're right. I guess we might as well stay and do some cleaning." Then she turns to me. "You can take off now, if you want to. You've done your duty."

"Well, I got nothing else to do. Might as well stay."

"Good, we can use the help," says the older woman. "My name is Betty. Terry is the guy in the other room."

"And Stephanie you've met," Ruthie adds, her mouth twitching. "Let's see your forehead," she says, grabbing my head firmly. "Not too bad. I don't think it needs stitches. Your mother's not gonna like it. You better call her."

"Yeah, guess I should."

"He'll sleep for a while," says Terry, coming out of the room as I dial.

"Hello, Billy? Is Mom there? Hey, Mom, I'm still at Benji's. No, I'm not drinking. Ruthie Garrell and some other folks are here. It's kind of a long story. We're helping him get cleaned up a little. I'll be home probably in a couple of hours. Oh, I got a call on my ad? Oh, that's good. No, really, it's great. I'll call them tomorrow."

"How can someone collect so much stuff?" asks Betty.

"It's always been like this," says Ruthie.

"What should we do with it?" says Stephanie.

"Burn it," says Terry.

"Really?" I ask.

"Really," says Ruthie.

A couple of hours later, as Betty stands at the sink drying dishes, Ruthie putting them away, and Terry mopping the floor, I follow Stephanie outside with a last bundle of newspapers for the old metal burn barrel out back.

"Place is starting to shape up," I say as I throw the newspapers into the burn barrel.

She smiles. "Surprised to see me here?"

"Yeah."

"We were on our way to a meeting."

"Ruthie had said earlier that she was going to take Benji to some kind of meeting."

"AA."

"I figured that's what she meant. Makes sense. Benji sure needs it."

She looks at me, raising her eyebrows.

"I was going, too," she says.

"Oh."

"For a smart guy, you aren't too bright. I go to meetings of Alcoholics Anonymous."

"Okay, why?"

"I have to. It's a long story."

"You said that once before, if I remember correctly."

"Well, it takes some time—"

"He has a right to know," says Ruthie, who has come up behind us.

Stephanie looks at Ruthie.

"Might as well tell him now," she says.

"I'm an addict," says Stephanie. "A junkie. Crack, heroin, cocaine, pot, booze, pretty much anything," says Stephanie matter-of-factly.

"You're not using now?"

"No, I'm not, one day at a time, as long as I go to meetings, I'm not. I've been clean a little more than a year."

"You just spent half a day with a drunk," says Ruthie. "Enjoy it?"

"Not particularly," I say defensively.

"She was worse," says Ruthie, waving her head toward Stephanie like a third-grade teacher pointing at a map on the wall. "You find that hard to believe?"

I stiffen. "Yeah, I find it hard to believe."

"Really? Well, fill him in," Ruthie says, turning to her niece.

"I started smoking pot when I was thirteen," she begins. "By the time I was fifteen, I was into coke and crack and then heroin. I was seventeen when I got pregnant with Samantha. I straightened out for a while, but even though I had a baby, I couldn't stay clean. I've stolen money, jewelry, televisions, computers, forged checks, shoplifted, and . . ." She hesitates and looks at Ruthie. ". . . and done time in jail."

"And that's the long version of your story?" I say to her.

"It's some of it; not all of it, but some."

"You still interested?" says Ruthie.

I just look at her.

Ruthie arches her eyebrows, turns to Stephanie, shakes her head slightly, and heads back to the house.

"What's her problem?"

"She's just very protective of me. She doesn't want to see me go back to what I was."

"And she thinks I'll cause you to go back?"

"No, it's just that getting into a relationship can, I don't know, can be dangerous."

"Dangerous? That's a little dramatic, isn't it?"

"Life is dramatic—and sometimes dangerous. It's not high school, going steady, romance for me anymore."

"You think it is for me?"

"I don't know what it is for you. I just know I have to be careful."

"I think we're about done," calls Ruthie as she walks down the porch steps.

"Should we say a prayer?" says Betty, following her down the steps.

Before I can protest, although I wasn't really about to say anything anyway, Stephanie slides her fingers across my palm and laces them into my fingers.

Betty grips the other hand, and Ruthie, across from me,

arches her eyebrows again.

"Our Father, who art in heaven . . .

Where do such words go? Who hears them?

". . . Amen."

seventeen

"So when I come back in," I say to Billy when he stops by the next morning, "he's got an envelope and a gun."

Billy looks toward the living room where Mom is vacuuming, and he shakes his head. "You're damned lucky," he says. "Does your mother know?"

"No, I didn't tell her about the gun. That would freak her out. Told her I tripped and fell."

"She believe you?"

I shrug my shoulders. "Probably not. I suppose I am lucky. I mean, I was scared, 'cause I did think he just might fire that thing. Not that he wanted to kill me. He was just—just drunk. He didn't know what the hell was going on."

"What was in the envelope?"

"A letter. An old one. He was carrying on about how he had old Mr. Garrick by the balls, because Garrick couldn't sell any of the land unless he agreed to it. So he gets this letter and shows it to me."

"You look at it?"

"Yeah, a little."

"And?"

"Well, from one of the paragraphs I read, it seems like maybe he has a point. He said the only other person he showed it to was

Dad. You ever hear about this?"

"Well, yeah, I've heard about a letter, but I didn't know anyone who had ever seen it. Your dad never told me that he had actually seen it."

"What do you make out of it?"

"I dunno. Could be something to it. Could be nothing. You just leave it there?"

"Yeah. On a table in the living room. He probably put it back. Like I said, he had it when he came out of the bathroom."

Billy finishes his coffee and smiles at Mom. "Pick you up around six thirty?" he says.

"Okay. You gonna join us?" she says to me.

"No, thanks. Not tonight."

"See ya," says Billy, kissing Mom on the cheek. Suddenly that kiss, which I've seen hundreds of times before, seems all wrong.

As Billy drives away, I ask, "Mom, does it bother you that Billy works for the state?"

"Bother me? Of course it doesn't bother me. Why should it? It's a good job. Does it bother you?"

"No, I guess not. At least, it never used to."

"What are you talking about?"

"I don't know. I mean, Garrick—"

"Frederick Garrick is an old fool."

"He's a smart man."

"All Garrick cares about is that land."

"That's his right, isn't it?"

"He should sell it to the state. He'd be a rich man."

"He doesn't want to. What did Dad think about it?"

"About what?"

"About the state and Garrick and Billy."

Mom pauses and looks at me. "What's this all about?"

"I dunno, maybe nothing. I told Billy about an old letter that Benji showed me last night. It was from Garrick's father to Benji's grandfather. Said neither could sell the land without the other one's permission."

She looks at me and then sits down slowly at the kitchen table.

"Your dad told me once about Benji's letter. He said he thought it probably wasn't what Benji thought it was—he doubted that it had much, if any, legal worth. That's all he said. I always wondered why he told me about it, but he asked me not to talk to anyone about it, and he never did either.

"Your father never cared much for politics," she says. "He didn't have much use for Garrick and his lawsuits, but he had less use for the state. In case you haven't noticed, a lot of people around here are poor. When the state condemned the land for state parks, people were forced to sell at what they figured was less than market value for their property. And besides, a lot of them didn't want to sell and move off the land they'd been on more than two or three generations. The state went after Garrick and his land, too, because he owned both sides of the river, and it is beautiful."

"You been up there?"

She smiles, recalling a memory. "Oh, I've been up there. Many times."

"Why didn't they get Garrick's land, too?"

"He had something the others didn't have—money and education."

"Yeah, and he's tough, too."

"He's tough, all right, but a lot of the people around here

are tough. Toughness alone isn't enough. So he fought, and still fights. I'm guessing he's pretty close to broke by now. Along the way, he's made a lot of enemies, and not just with the state. Most of the people around here couldn't care less if the state got his land. They figure if they had to sell, so should he."

"What about Benji?"

"What about him?"

"Benji and Dad?"

"Your father always had a soft spot for Benji. When they were kids."

"What happened?"

"We got married. You came along. Benji kept drinking, your dad didn't."

"And Billy?"

She doesn't answer.

"You have other plans for tonight?" she says to me, changing the subject.

"Maybe."

"They wouldn't involve that waitress, would they?"

"Maybe."

"She's got a little girl, you know."

"Yeah, I know."

eighteen

"Hello."

"Danny?"

"Hey. I was wondering if you might call."

"I've only got a few minutes. I've got to run."

"Where to?"

"A meeting."

"Oh. You go to them every night?"

"Pretty much."

"Oh. How long do you have to keep going? Do you, like, graduate or something?"

"Uh, no. There's no graduation. You just keep going."

"Forever?"

"Well, yeah, I guess so. Ruthie's been sober about fourteen years, and she still goes. I've met people who have been going for more than twenty-five years. So I guess it is forever. I haven't thought much about it."

"What are these meetings like? I mean, well, what do you do there?"

"Hard to explain. If you're interested, you can go to one with me sometime."

"Would they let me in? I mean, I'm not, well, you know, I'm not—"

"An addict? Like me?"

"I didn't mean it like that."

"It's okay. I'm not offended. There are open meetings for people who aren't addicts. You could go with me to one of them. You interested?"

"Well, I guess so. I mean, can't hurt, can it?"

"Who knows, you might learn something about Kaitlyn with a K, and why you quit school."

Silence.

"It was a little joke," Stephanie says.

"Right."

"I seem to have hit a nerve."

"You called me up just to remind me what a jerk I am?"

"No, I'm sorry. I didn't mean to get you mad, really."

"Don't worry about it."

"No, really, I'm sorry. I called to see if you might like to get together tomorrow."

"Yeah, I would like that. That would be great."

"Well, I've got tons of homework, so I don't have a lot of time, but I would like to see you."

"I'll sit and watch you do homework."

"That sounds like fun."

"It would be for me."

"Aren't we romantic?"

"I could just sit and stare."

"Sounds boring."

"Not from my point of view."

"Can you put that in a song?"

"Major or minor key?"

"A love song has to be in a minor key."

"So what time should I show up?"

Pause.

"Well, we go to Mass at ten. You want to join us?" she asks quietly.

"You mean at church?"

"It's the thing with a steeple."

"I know, it's just that—"

"What?"

"I don't go to church."

"Ever?"

"Well, once in a while, but it's been years."

"Well, it won't hurt you."

"What church?"

"St. John's."

"Is that a Catholic church?"

"Yes. Does it matter?"

"No, it's just that I've never been in a Catholic church. I won't know what to do."

"Well, you won't be alone. You'll be with us. We'll tell you what to do. You have to stand sometimes, and sometimes you have to kneel. The sermon is short, but the new priest, a guy named Father Stephen, is really something special. So, what do you think?"

"Okay, I'll be there," I say.

"I'll meet you about fifteen minutes before ten," she says.

"Sounds good."

"I'll see you then."

"Bye," I say as Mom and Billy come in.

"Bye."

"Who was that?" asks Mom.

"Stephanie."

"That's her name?" she asks.

"Yeah."

"The waitress?" asks Billy.

I nod slightly.

"You don't waste any time, do you?" he says.

"You want a cup of coffee?" Mom says to him.

"Nah, I got an early day tomorrow."

"It's Sunday. You're not working, are you?" she asks.

"Nope. Goin' fishin'. You wanna join me, Danny?"

"Gonna be busy tomorrow."

"Nothing much better than trout fishing on an April morning, unless, of course, it involves a woman." He looks at Mom. "See ya," he says.

"She asked me to go to church with her tomorrow," I say, turning to Mom. "You believe that? I'm going to church."

"It can't hurt you," says Mom.

"That's what she said."

"Smart girl. I could never get you to go."

"Didn't we used to go?"

"We did."

"How is it that we stopped going, anyway?"

"Well, if you'll recall, it was always a battle to get you to go, and your father refused to go."

"How come?"

"'God is in the all-outdoors,' he would say, 'not in a building with some preacher telling you what to believe.' I couldn't change him, and after a while, the battle with you got to be too difficult. You won."

"How come you stopped going?"

"I just stopped, that's all."

"Did it have to do with Dad dying?"

"No, I don't think so. I think I had stopped before that."

"But him dying didn't make you go back to church, either, did it?"

"No."

nineteen

"I've always been fascinated with this story about the woman taken in adultery.

"There're a couple of things that always strike me about this story. Tradition has it that the woman was a prostitute, which she was not; and later, one of the popes said the woman was Mary Magdalene, who she was not.

"But the one thing we do know is that the witnesses say that Jesus wrote something on the ground with His forefinger, as though He had not heard her accusers, before He says anything.

"Nobody knows what He wrote, but it had to be important; otherwise, why include it in the story?

"In fact, it is so important that after He accuses Mary's accusers by saying, 'Let him who is without sin among you be the first to throw a stone at her,' He then writes on the ground a second time.

"Jesus twice writes in the earth—on Mother Earth—before He speaks to the sinning woman.

"'Woman, where are they?' He asks her. 'Has no one condemned you?' And she says, 'No one, Lord.' And Jesus says to her, 'Neither do I condemn you.'

"What an insight into the hypocrisy of men and their dealings with women and the power of God to heal that rupture.

"The condemned sons of Adam used her, then condemned her, and would have killed her had it not been for the power of the True Man, the Son of God, who first writes on the face of Mother Earth.

"And then with a scathing accusation—'Let him who is without sin among you be the first to throw a stone at her'—vanquishes the hypocrites and would-be executioners to rescue the fallen woman, not only from physical death but, surely and more importantly, from spiritual death. Then Jesus says to her—and this is the line that is often conveniently forgotten—'Go and do not sin again.'

"'Go,' He tells her, 'and do not sin again.'

"I wonder if that is possible? To 'go and do not sin again'? I think perhaps it is. But to do so would require superhuman, supernatural help. We don't know for sure whether the woman taken in adultery does not sin again. The mark of true and complete conversion is, to some degree, not sinning. Not sinning would be to exist in a state of grace. I think Mary Magdalene, when she saw the risen Christ, must have been in such a state.

"Do we really want to know God the way Mary Magdalene knew God? Really? Then we must do as He commanded the adulterous woman to do: 'Go and do not sin again.' But how is it possible to do that?

"I said that I thought it was possible, but only if one first sees that it is not possible. It is not possible unless we are desperate enough—like the adulterous woman—to wish to hear the healing words of God. Desperation—fearing for your life, fearing for your soul—comes from suffering, because only suffering will bring us to surrendering.

"Those who have truly heard the words of God, heard the

words deep in their soul, so that their entire being is changed, have all paid one price. They have suffered. But suffering isn't something you have to go out and find. We are all suffering. This culture of ours suffers. We spend our lives trying to avoid, cover up, remain ignorant to, run away from, anesthetize, and medicate suffering. We are asleep to the reality of suffering. If we would, in the words of Christ, 'Wake up!' we would be desperate, and then we could be healed by the words of God."

twenty

"This is Danny, Father. Danny Murtaugh."

"Murtaugh? Don't I know that name?"

I look at Stephanie, stumped as to what I'm supposed to say.

"Danny's father died in a drowning accident years ago," Ruthie tells him.

"Oh, I'm sorry," says Father Stephen.

"It was a long time ago," I say.

"But you're not Catholic, are you?"

His question catches me off guard. "No," I say quickly.

"Forgive me for asking. I'm new here, you know, and I think there is a Mass being said soon in honor of your father, but you're not Catholic, right?"

"No, I'm not."

"Well, I guess I'm a little confused. Perhaps I've made a mistake."

"No, Father, I think someone does have a Mass said for Danny's father each year at the anniversary of his death," says Ruthie.

"Oh, well, I hope you'll join us then," he says.

"Someone has a Mass said for my father?" I ask Ruthie as we head down the church steps.

"You didn't know that?"

"No. Who has the Mass said?"

"I don't know. It always says Anonymous on the church bulletin," Ruthie answers. "So, what did you think about our church?" she asks, changing the subject.

"Well—" I start to say, but then nothing follows.

"Oh, come on, be honest," she says.

"Well, church is—confining."

"Confining. That's different. But I suppose true."

"I like to be outside. I guess I'm like my father."

"Your father was an unusual man," Ruthie says. "He had everybody's respect. He was the kind of guy if anybody needed something, they'd ask your dad, and he would do it, most of the time for free. It drove your mom nuts, but I think that's what she loved about him, too. Just about everybody in this town has a story about him helpin' them."

We walk over to our cars.

"I was planning on going up into the woods later today to take some pictures," I say to both of them. "You wanna join me?"

"Not me," says Ruthie. "I'm too old, and besides, you really mean Stephanie, anyway."

"No, really—"

Ruthie just smiles.

"Okay. Stephanie, do you want to join me?"

Stephanie looks at Ruthie.

"Yeah, I can take care of Samantha," she says. "Go."

twenty-one

"What's that you're playing?"

"Something I'm working on," I say, looking up at my mother.

"It's beautiful."

"Thanks."

"What's it called?"

"No name yet. Just variations in D."

"I haven't heard you play in more than two months, and here you are sitting down, just composing a little something in D. It's gorgeous."

"A lot of church hymns are written in D."

"One day in church and you're becoming an expert."

"No, Mom, we had to study this stuff in college."

"Well, I'm glad you learned something in the short time you were there."

"Don't start, okay?"

My mother sighs and falls into the big chair by the piano that occupies most of the little living room of our two-bedroom house.

"Danny, what are you doing with your life?"

"Mom, please."

"We can't avoid this conversation."

I stop playing. The muscles in my neck tense like they did when Benji grabbed me.

"We need to talk, Danny."

"What do you want from me, Mom? I can't go back to school. Not just yet."

"Okay. When?"

"I don't know."

"Danny, I know this isn't fair of me, but I've got to say it anyway. I worked two jobs to help pay for your lessons. They weren't cheap. Neither was driving you down to the city each week for a better part of two years. If it wasn't for the extra money from your grandfather and your teacher letting you stay at his house, we couldn't have done it."

"I didn't ask you to do all that."

"Don't even go there!"

"Whaddaya mean, 'don't go there'! I'm not the one who asked to be a piano player."

"You didn't? The hell you didn't! You begged us to get a piano."

"I was seven years old, for God's sake. You can't hold that against me."

"I don't hold it against you."

"The hell you don't. Your whole point is why I'm not living up to your expectations of me, because I wanted to play the piano."

"You're not making any sense."

"I'm making a lot of sense. I'm sick of playing the piano just because you want me to get out of this town, have a different life. Different from what? I don't know what I want. I really don't know. But I know what I don't want. I don't want you running my life anymore!"

She rubs her face and pushes her fingers through her hair. "I give up. I really do. Do what you want. But I'll tell you this, you can't live here forever. I've got a life to live, too, you know."

"Yeah, well, so do I," I say, grabbing my jacket and walking out the door.

"Where are you going?"

"I got a date, believe it or not."

"Be careful."

"What's that supposed to mean?"

"Jesus! It just means be careful."

"Be careful—as in, don't get her pregnant and ruin your whole life."

twenty-two

"Mr. Garrick?" I say as he comes to the door. "I'd like you to meet a friend of mine."

"I'm in the middle—" then he pauses and looks at Stephanie. "I can take a few minutes. Come in."

"It's loaded," I whisper to Stephanie as she glances down at the gun on the table.

"Can I get you something to drink? Lemonade? Pepsi?"

I look at Stephanie to see if we're going to stay for a little while. "Lemonade is fine," she says.

"Daniel?"

"Same for me, Mr. Garrick."

"Well, this is a pleasant surprise," he says, handing us the glasses. "I was just noting all of the endangered or threatened species that live on my land—the state will have to account for each of them in any environmental-impact study they propose."

Stephanie looks at me as though I'm going to explain this to her, but since I don't know exactly what Garrick is talking about, I say nothing.

"Why does the state need to do a study?" she finally asks.

Garrick laughs. "Well, young lady, because they want my land. They want to condemn it and take it, but if they take someone's land when the owner doesn't want to sell, then they have to give very good reasons why they're taking it."

The smile on his face fades, and he stares toward the woods beyond his back porch. "This owner doesn't want to sell, and those sons of bitches aren't going to get this land of mine without a fight."

He turns back to Stephanie; the smile returns. "So they're going to have to file an environmental-impact study, and they are going to have to account for each and every one of the rattle-snakes, eagles, beaver, mink, weasels, coyotes, wolves, bobcats, and other animals that make my land their home. Not to mention the hundreds of plant species.

"So, what brings you up here today, Daniel? You have more photos for me?"

"No, sir, not with me. Actually, I know you gave me permission to be on your property, but I'd like to take Stephanie for a walk, so I wanted to see if that would be okay."

"That's professional . . . and smart," says Garrick. "Permission granted."

"Thank you."

"I've heard wonderful things about your land," says Stephanie. "I can't wait to see it firsthand."

"Well, you can't see it all in one day. Not walking. Why don't you take the old Jeep. It runs okay, and you can see more of it. Come here, let me show you something on the map. I don't think you've ever seen this, Danny. Just before you get to the end of my drive, there's a trail through the woods on the left. It'll take you down into a valley and then up a steep incline. When you get to the top, you'll see some blueberry bushes on your right and some huge rhododendrons about fifty yards beyond. There's a path that heads up to a peak, and as you get toward the top, you'll see something that will take your breath away. A quirk of nature, perhaps, but you'll know it, because it's a gateway into heaven.

"Follow me. Sometimes the Jeep is a little hard to start."

As we walk toward the garage I notice a small gravestone set off near the woods with the name Roman engraved on it.

"Roman," I say. "Isn't that the name of the dog that my dad saved?"

Garrick looks at me, expressionless.

"When did he die?" I say.

"He died that day. I shot him."

twenty-three

"I think you better slow down," she says, after another jarring bump. "My head hit the roof on that one."

"What?"

"Slow down!"

"Too fast?"

"Danny, what's the matter? You're driving like crazy, and you haven't spoken a word since we left the house."

I stop the Jeep in the middle of the path and stare at her. "He shot the dog. My father saved that dog, and that son of a bitch shot him—he died for nothing."

"What happened? I mean, I heard he drowned."

"When I was nine. It had been raining a lot—the tail end of a hurricane down South. We went for a walk down to the river, near where Garrick's river comes into the big river. I saw a dog in the river and started yelling. My dad went in to get the dog."

"I'm sorry."

"Well, it was a long time ago. I don't think about it much, if at all. My dad died of a heart attack onshore."

"You saw it."

"Yeah."

"I think," she says, after a long pause, "Garrick shot the dog because it would always remind him of what happened. He killed the dog because he felt guilty. It was his dog, and he couldn't stand to have the guilt looking him in the face every day."

"Then why'd he give the stupid dog a monument?"

"I don't know."

"The dog's still dead—and so is my father," I say as I drive up the ridge toward the path that Garrick described.

"That's true, and Mr. Garrick can't hide from his feelings about it by shooting a dog. And you can't hide from your feelings, either."

"What's that supposed to mean?"

"I don't know. All I know is that you're messed up. You have a full scholarship to a music school, and you're not there. And it's not because of what's-her-name."

"Kaitlyn."

"Right, Kaitlyn, with a K," she says with a sly smile.

"What are you laughing about?"

"Nothing. Well, it's just how easy guys are to play."

"That's reassuring. I think this is the path," I say as I pull the Jeep off near some bushes. "So now it's my turn to psychoanalyze you."

"What?"

"Well, you had your shot at figuring out some Freudian thing about me and my father. So now it's my turn."

"Okay, doctor, tell me my troubles. What have you discovered about me?"

"Okay. What about Ruthie?"

"Ruthie?"

"She's kinda like your mother, isn't she?"

"What?"

"Ruthie. She's not your mother, but like your mother, right?"

"Yeah, she is. Technically, she's my dad's sister. You're wondering why I don't live with my parents?"

"Well, yeah."

"Another long story."

"We got time," I say, motioning toward a path running uphill through the red tips of early spring blueberry bushes.

"I did a lot of things to hurt them," she says. "Stole from them. Yelled at them. Punched them. It wasn't pleasant to live with a junkie."

"They oughta be proud of you—watch out for the thorns on this," I say, holding back a prickly branch of a young locust tree as Stephanie ducks under my hand.

"Actually, it was when I started to get straight that things got worse," she says. "It's weird. They were used to me using. I wasn't much of a mother, if at all. So they stepped in to raise Samantha. They were becoming her parents. I was just this cloud of darkness that they tolerated, because I had this child. When I got straight, I decided I had to be a good mom, too. They weren't used to me trying to be responsible. They didn't think I had a right to be Samantha's mother. One day, a little more than a year ago, they had some papers for me to sign. They're quite wealthy. Had their lawyer draw up a contract. The contract basically said they'd set me up for life, but I had to give up custody of Samantha to them. I freaked out. Started screaming at them. I didn't know what to do, so I called Ruthie. She told me it was time for me to leave and said I could live with her."

"No more contact with your parents?"

"Leaving wasn't easy. They literally blocked the door. I had to threaten to call the police on them."

"So here you are," I say, looking at her.

"Yeah, here I am."

"Here we are," I say with a smile.

"Yes, here we are." She smiles back.

Face-to-face in the middle of the woods.

"So, just where are we, anyway?" she says, turning her head from my eyes and looking beyond me into the distance.

"Well," I say, following her look, "I think we're near where Garrick said we would see the 'gateway to heaven.'"

"How much farther?"

"Just a little bit, I think. There are the rhododendrons. I'm surprised there's not more snow up here this time of year. We probably couldn't get through without boots. But it's been such a light winter, there's no snow at all. Just over this hill."

We slide and slosh through the broken frozen ground, thawing in the early April sun. The air rising from the cold earth, slowly waking to another spring.

I step to the crest of a small rise on the path and pause. I touch her hand and gently pull her alongside of me.

"Oh my God!" she says.

There on a ridge in the distance stand two huge fir trees, side by side. The right side of the tree on the right, fully grown; the left side of the tree on the left, also full of green. But in the middle, an opening about thirty yards wide, so that the blue sky hangs like a canopy on the tips of the firs and pine trees beyond the two great trees.

"How is it—" Stephanie begins.

"Lightning."

"Lightning?"

"Look at the sides of the trees. It must have happened a long time ago. It's just like Garrick said, a 'gateway into heaven.' A perfect opening into—"

"Into what?" she says.

"I don't know," I say, looking at her face.

"God?"

"Yeah, I suppose. Into God—and God's creatures," I say, my hand reaching to touch her face.

Softly she puts her hand on mine and stops me.

"Why are you interested in me?" she says.

"What?"

"Why are you interested in me?" she repeats.

"What are you talking about?"

"We barely know each other."

"Well, we know something about each other."

"Barely. But why are you interested in me?"

"Because you're beautiful."

"I have a daughter."

"So?"

"I am an addict."

"You're not now."

"I've been in jail."

"So?"

"That doesn't matter?"

"Stephanie, I can't figure you out."

"Are you supposed to?"

"What?"

"Figure me out."

"I just wanted to go for a walk and—"

"And what?"

Silence.

"And—I don't know—enjoy your company."

"How quaint," she says, walking toward the two huge evergreens.

"Okay, now I've got a question for you. Why are you interested in me?"

She turns back to look at me. "You're safe," she says as she walks on.

"Safe?"

"Yes, safe."

"What is that supposed to mean?"

She stops and shakes her head no, but doesn't answer.

"What does 'safe' mean?" I repeat, catching up to her.

"'Safe' means just that. You're cute. Interesting. Talented."

"And safe?"

"Yeah. Nothing's going to happen."

"How do you know?"

"I know."

"Maybe I'll surprise you, and you'll fall in love with me."

Stephanie reaches up and lightly touches my cheek with her fingers. "No, not love."

"Have you been in love?"

She doesn't answer.

"Samantha's father?"

"Sean?"

"That's his name?"

"Yeah, Sean. In love with Sean? Hardly."

"Where is he?"

"Jail. I think. I hope."

"Oh. I'm sorry."

"I'm not. If I'm lucky, Samantha will never see him."

"Never know him?"

"Sound cruel?" she says.

"Well, I kinda know something about that, you know, not knowing your father."

"This is different. He's a scumbag."

"How did—"

"The same way everyone does. It just had nothing to do with love. One of the lovely features of living the life of a junkie is living life with other junkies. That's all Sean was. Is."

"Have you ever been in love?" I ask.

"I don't know. I don't think so. Were you in love with Kaitlyn?"

"I thought I was. But probably not. Just infatuation."

"Dependency?" she says, her sarcastic smile nipping at the corners of her mouth.

"S'pose."

"Like a puppy dog." The smile fades. "That's why you're safe."

"What are you talking about?"

"I meet you while I'm playing the piano. We have coffee. I see you out at Benji's. We go to church. We end up in the woods. What the hell am I thinking?"

"I don't understand."

"Ruthie was right. I can't do this."

"Do what? What are you talking about?"

"I have a three-year-old daughter! I'm not in high school anymore. Those days are gone for me, if they were ever there."

Bam!

"What was that?"

"Gunshot," I say.

"Hunters?"

"Too early for turkey hunters, and besides, they'd be using shotguns. That was a pistol shot."

"Benji?"

"Maybe. Could be Garrick. He uses a pistol to hunt woodchucks."

"Is Benji's house far from here?"

"No."

"Shouldn't we better go check?"

Reluctantly, or maybe relieved, I nod my head yes. But as I turn to walk past Stephanie back down the path, she grabs my arm.

"I'm sorry. I haven't been with a guy for more than a year. It's a promise I made to Ruthie and to myself. I don't know how to act. I used to know, or I thought I knew."

Then she kisses me.

twenty-four

The wooden pine steps creak.

"Benji!" I holler, stepping onto the porch. "I hope he's not drunk," I say to Stephanie.

"Benji," echoes Stephanie, knocking on the screen door. "Should we go in?"

"S'pose we have to—Benji, it's me, Danny."

"Benji—not here?" she says as we walk into the house. "What happened to the house we cleaned? This place is a mess."

"Didn't take him long to get things back the way he likes them. Benji," I call again. "I'll check the bedrooms and bathroom."

"I'll check out back," she says as I head into the bathroom.

"Danny! Come quick! I found him!"

Sprawled, facedown on the stone walkway, his feet hanging over the last two steps of the back staircase, pistol in his right hand, a pool of blood beneath his head, lies Benjamin Samuels.

"Is he dead?" asks Stephanie.

I lift Benji's limp wrist. "No pulse. I think so."

"We need to call someone, don't we?"

"Yeah, the police, I guess. When you hollered for me, I was about to call for you. The bathroom and the bedroom are a mess. It seems to me that it's way too messed up for Benji to have done this so soon."

"What do you mean? You think someone was here?"

"I could be wrong, but it sure looks that way."

"I think we better call the police."

"Yeah, and I think I'd better call Garrick, too."

twenty-five

"You should have called me first," Garrick says. "The police are going to ask a lot of questions. This was no accident."

"What do you mean?" says Stephanie.

Garrick looks coldly at Stephanie but doesn't answer.

"You don't think the state had anything to do . . . ," I ask.

"They're always up here looking around," he says. Then his eyes narrow, and he stares at me. "You know something, Daniel, don't you?"

"Benji showed me a letter between his grandfather and your father about the land."

"Go on."

"I mentioned it to Billy."

"Billy? Billy Taylor?"

"Yes."

"Why didn't you just e-mail the state park commissioner?" he says sarcastically.

"Billy wouldn't do this."

"Wouldn't he? You don't know him very well, do you?" he says, glaring at me.

"Do you think they found it?" I say, trying to break his stare.

"What? The letter?"

"Yes."

"It doesn't matter if they did or not. It's worthless."

"But Benji said—"

"Benji liked to delude himself that the letter had some value."

"He showed it to me."

"It wasn't a legal document," says Garrick matter-of-factly. "My father and his grandfather had an idea about building a dam on the river and creating a huge lake. All the letter said was that if they ever did such a thing, each of them would have some say about who got what. Benji's grandfather ran into some cash problems, and my father bought out Benji's family, with the stipulation that the Samuelses could live here as long as there was a Samuels' heir. The letter means nothing—unfortunately, Billy Taylor is too stupid to know that. Benji died for nothing," he says.

Tires on the soft dirt, engines coming to a halt, fumes of exhaust, car doors click open and slam shut.

"Don't volunteer anything they don't ask for," he says.

"Anyone in there?" a voice from outside asks.

Garrick nods to me to answer.

"Yeah, we're in here," I say.

In walk two state troopers, a plainclothes detective, three local cops, ambulance people, a man in a suit, and a couple of state park rangers. About a dozen men in all. The only one I recognize is Peter Thompson, Billy's boss.

"Mr. Garrick," says the man in the suit. "I'm surprised to see you here."

"No, you're not," says Garrick.

The man smiles but says nothing in response.

"Why the army?" says Garrick.

"The body's out back?" asks one of the state troopers.

"Have you moved it or touched it?" asks another.

"No," I say, "except to check his pulse."

"What's your name?" a trooper says, looking at me.

"Danny Murtaugh."

"And yours?" he says to Stephanie.

"Stephanie Sanders."

"Yours?" he says to Garrick.

Garrick turns his head, ignoring the question.

"Frederick P. Garrick," says the man in the suit. "You are talking to Frederick P. Garrick."

"Whose land you're on without permission," snaps Garrick.

"We don't need permission," says one of the state park rangers.

Garrick looks right into the man's eyes. "I seem to have left my gun in my Jeep," Garrick says to the man.

"Is that a threat?" the man says.

"A fact. I never threaten. I only state facts," Garrick says, turning back to the man in the suit. "You're on my land without permission. Produce a warrant or leave."

"Mr. Garrick," says the plainclothes detective, "we're considering this a possible homicide, so for the time being, we need to be here to investigate."

"A homicide? Now who would want to kill a defenseless old man who lives alone in the woods?" says Garrick sarcastically.

"That's what we're trying to find out," says the detective. "Can you step into the other room?" he says to me.

"No, he can't," says Garrick quickly, stopping me before I can even stand up.

"We need to talk to him," says the detective.

"You can talk out here, to all three of us," says Garrick.

"I prefer to talk to each of you individually."

"I prefer you talk to all of us together."

"You're not running this investigation, so what you prefer doesn't matter," says the detective.

"Let me see," says Garrick. "Today is Sunday. My attorney would be a little hard to contact, but I suppose he could be here in maybe two or three hours, and in the meantime, we prefer not to talk."

"You're obstructing—"

"No, I'm not, and you know it. You're not charging us with anything. We don't even have to talk to you, but we'll be nice and cooperate, but we'll do it together."

The man in the suit laughs.

"Okay, Mr. Garrick, we'll talk to all three of you, out here, together," says the detective.

twenty-six

"Could you tell us exactly what happened?" says the detective.

"We were going for a walk," I begin.

"We? You and Ms. Sanders?"

"Yes. We were about half a mile away through the woods when we heard a shot. We thought it was coming from Benji's house, so we came here as quickly as possible."

"Did you see anyone else in the woods?"

"No."

"Then what?"

"We called for Benji when we got here. He didn't answer. We came inside. The house was a mess and since we had just cleaned it . . ."

"Just cleaned it?"

"It's a long story, but a few of us were here the other night and we cleaned the house. And already it was a mess. When I looked around, it seemed to me that Benji couldn't have messed it up that quickly."

"And then?"

"Stephanie went out back and called to me that she had found Benji."

"He was lying facedown," says Stephanie, "just like he is now. There was a lot of blood. I called for Danny."

"I checked for a pulse, but I couldn't find any. We came inside. Called the police and called Mr. Garrick."

"Anything else?"

"No."

"That's it then. I'll need you two to read this over," says the detective. "And if it's correct, I'll need you to sign this."

He hands me the statement as one of the troopers hands him a note.

"Ms. Sanders," he says, looking up from the note, "may I speak with you in private?"

"No, she—" begins Mr. Garrick, but the detective cuts him off.

"Ms. Sanders?"

Stephanie shakes her head no.

"You're sure?"

"I'm sure," she says.

"Okay." He pauses, then says, "Have you ever been arrested?"

"Yes," she says.

"Obviously, you know she has, or else you wouldn't have asked," says Garrick. "What does this have to do with Mr. Samuels's death?"

"Are you on probation?"

"No. Not anymore."

"Well, Ms. Sanders, we just ran a check on you, and according to the records, your probation in New Jersey doesn't end until September. You're not supposed to be in New York. Do you realize that you have broken your probation terms?"

"What are you talking about? I had a hearing in December. They told me they dropped the charges."

"What were you arrested for?"

Stephanie fidgets. "Shoplifting and forging checks," she says.

The detective looks down at the note.

I look at Stephanie, wondering what's going on. Her eyes stare straight at the detective. No anger. No hatred. Just a stare.

"Ah, Ms. Sanders, this violation is for prostitution."

The men in the room stop and stare, and so do I.

"That's it!" yells Garrick, jumping to his feet. "You're finished! Get off my land! Get off my land now, or I'll sue every one of you sons of bitches for everything you've got!"

"Ms. Sanders," says the detective, "I'm afraid you'll have to come with us to get this straightened out."

"Yeah," she whispers.

I stand on the porch, watching the police lead her away. I don't say a word. Not "Good-bye." Not "I'll call Ruthie." Not "I'll follow you." Nothing. Paralyzed.

In the background, as I watch Stephanie walk away, dull voices fill the silence surrounding the death of Benjamin Samuels.

"You have all the photos you need?" yells one voice.

"Yeah. Got everything."

"Fingerprints?"

"Got 'em."

"Okay, put the body in the ambulance. Let's go."

As the cars pull away through the forest, Garrick turns to me. "Daniel, find a phone book and get the number for Thomas Brothers and St. John's Church. We need to make arrangements for Benjamin's burial and funeral."

Dutifully, I walk toward the phone. A prostitute, I think. I look down and see the photo of my father holding that big trout.

"Daniel?"

"Yeah," I say, still staring at the photo.

"Are you going to call?"

"Yeah, sorry."

Garrick walks over and looks down at the photo.

"Benji showed it to me," I say to Garrick. "Told me I could have it when he died. Said it was the best summer he ever had. He told me your brother took the photo."

Garrick says nothing.

"You have a brother?"

He turns away. "Make the call."

twenty-seven

"They said she had broken probation," I say to Ruthie.

"Broken probation? She had a hearing last year. I was there. She's not on probation anymore."

"They said this was for a different charge than the shop-lifting."

"What? Forging checks? That was rolled into the same hearing."

"No."

"What then?"

"Ah . . ."

"What?"

"Prostitution."

"Damn. She told me the charges had been dropped more than a year ago. Ah, shit. Well, I better go get her."

Ruthie walks over toward her car and looks back at me.

"You comin'?"

"Yeah."

"A little surprise, heh?" Ruthie says as we drive away.

"What?"

"Prostitution. Not what you expected."

"No, not what I expected."

"It takes a long time to outlive the past."

"I suppose."

Silence.

"Men are so stupid," she says, lighting a cigarette. "It's always all about sex."

"Not all . . ."

"Don't bother. You know damn well it's true. Don't tell me it's about love and finding the one girl. 'Cause while you're out trying to find the right one, you're all screwin' anything that's alive, breathing, and wears a dress. Although the dress is apparently optional."

"What are you so pissed off about?"

We pull into the police station.

"I get scared for her. And Samantha. It's a hard life. I've had it hard. She's had it hard. You've had it hard, too. When things like this happen," she says, nodding toward the police station, "it scares the hell out of me. Just when you think the past is over and gone, it comes up and bites you in the ass."

Inside, we find Stephanie. Thin, frail, a waif. Her foot tapping. She looks up. The mascara has smeared, and her eyes, outlined in black, are sunken and ghoulish.

"Gimme a cigarette," she says to Ruthie.

"No, you quit."

"Gimme a fuckin' cigarette, now."

"Don't you speak to me like that! I'm not some low-life friend of yours. Knock it off!"

Fear and rage explode into tears. She falls into Ruthie's arms. She sobs. I stand there, not knowing what to do, wondering how to leave quickly and quietly.

Finally, Stephanie pulls back from the embrace.

"This too shall pass," says Ruthie.

Stephanie wipes the blackened tears on her face and nods.

"What did they tell you?" says Ruthie.

"They said they'd try to get in touch with my probation officer, but it's Sunday, so, of course, they're not going to get anyone."

"Well, let me go see what I can find out," says Ruthie, standing up.

So I stand there, and Stephanie looks up at me.

"You wanna leave yet?" she says quietly.

"No, I think I'll stay." I sit down.

"I thought the charges had been dropped."

I nod.

Stephanie stares, away from the clutter of the people and the piles of paper sitting on the police desk, into memories of a life I've only seen glimpses of on TV. "I only did it a few times," she whispers. "Mostly money for drugs."

She turns to me and looks into my eyes. "It's disgusting. Degrading. A man doesn't understand. But—"

"They're going to release you to my custody. They set an appearance date in a month. By that time we'll be able to contact your probation officer, the judge, and get this cleared up. Come on, sweetie," Ruthie says as she gathers Stephanie into her arms. "Let's go home. Your daughter's waiting."

twenty-eight

For the second time in a week I am in a church. I haven't been in church in years, and now twice in one week. This time with my mother; Stephanie and Ruthie are in front of us. There are more people than I thought there would be at Benji's funeral. And sitting in the front row, alone, is Frederick P. Garrick. He must be Catholic. He seems to know what to do.

Father Stephen walks toward us. He talks to Stephanie. Then she turns around to me, and he looks into my eyes.

"Danny, I hate to ask you this, but Margaret, the organist, is sick and can't play," she says.

"Her sister just called," says Father Stephen. "They had to take Margaret to the hospital."

"I'm sorry to hear that," I say mechanically.

"Stephanie tells me you're quite accomplished."

"I play the piano, not the organ," I protest.

"We have a piano. That would be fine," he says.

"But I don't know what to do, where to come in."

"I'll sit with you and guide you through it," says Stephanie.

My mother puts her hand on my shoulder. She doesn't have to say anything.

And Ruthie gives me one of her looks, too.

"Okay. Okay."

So I slide onto a bench in front of an old upright Wurlitzer.

"Is it in tune?" I whisper to Stephanie.

"Beats me. You'll find out soon enough."

Father Stephen pokes his head out from the hallway near us.

"What hymn do you wish to start with?" he says.

"I don't know. You tell me."

"'Amazing Grace'?"

"Fine."

"Keep it simple," says Stephanie.

"Gotcha," I smile.

"I did not know Benjamin Samuels," Father Stephen begins after the hymn, "so it would be presumptuous of me to proceed as though he and I were old friends or even acquaintances. But some of you did know him, and I thought what we might do is take some time to ask a few of you to say some words about him. A story, a memory, a thought."

Then he sits down and waits in silence.

This is risky. S'pose nobody stands up and says anything. What do we do, sit in silence?

I hear some movement, and Ruthie stands up.

"The two things Benji liked to do was fish and drink," she says. "Maybe not in that order, though."

People chuckle.

One after one, people stand and talk about Benji Samuels. People laughing, crying, talking about life, about death.

When they are finished, after a moment's pause, Father Stephen says, "Please stand and sing. . . ." He looks at me.

"'Be Still, My Soul,'" says Stephanie. "'Finlandia,'" she whispers to me.

I play through one verse. The notes rise from the old Wurlitzer and hang heavy like tree moss in the church air.

Her lips breathe in, and sweet and softly she sings: "Be still, my soul, the Lord is on thy side; bear patiently the cross of grief or pain."

twenty-nine

Tears are warm when they run down your neck. And perfume seems sweeter when a girl cries in your arms. Her body trembles and heaves and sighs, and men, I think, don't know what to do. Words seem foolish, because they are. And even a simple stroke on her hair and a pat on her back is stupid. But it's the best we can do, I guess.

I don't know if she was crying for Benji, or for herself, or for all of us. I think the tears are what we're supposed to do. But they don't come for me. And I suppose I feel guilty about that. Shouldn't I cry? Most people do. But not everyone.

Frederick P. Garrick just sits and says nothing.

"You did a great job," Ruthie says to me.

"Thanks for your help," says Father Stephen.

"Here," says Garrick, handing Father Stephen an envelope. "It should be enough to cover expenses for this and more. I'd like a Mass said for him on the anniversary of his death for as long as this is good. You did a good job today. If you need money for something important, come and see me. Just don't be greedy."

"I'll make sure the Masses are said," says Father Stephen.

"Good."

Outside, I find myself with my mother and Ruthie and

Stephanie on the steps of the church.

"Quite a service," says Ruthie to Mom.

"Yes, it was," she replies. "Brings back a lot of memories."

"Yes, it does," says Ruthie. "Not all of them pleasant."

"No, I suppose not."

"Too bad Billy—"

"I think he had to work," Mom says defensively.

"It is good to see you, Linda," says Ruthie.

"You, too," says Mom, and I can see she's trying to say something else, but it can't quite come out.

"You got time for a slice of pizza?" I say suddenly to Stephanie.

"No, I've got to get home to Samantha."

"I'll take care of her when I get home," says Ruthie. "You should go."

"I don't—"

"Go," says Ruthie emphatically.

"Okay, but I don't have too much time," she says to me. "I have to work the evening shift later at the diner. Let me get changed. I'll meet you in about fifteen minutes."

"She's beautiful," says Mom as Stephanie and Ruthie walk away.

"Yeah, she is."

thirty

"Hop in the back," I say to Jasper as I open the door to the red pickup truck for Stephanie.

As soon as I get behind the wheel she says, "I think we better end this."

"Whaddaya mean? Whaddaya talking about?"

"This," she says, pointing back and forth to each of us. "You and me. This this."

"Why?"

"It's not going to work. We should be honest about it before it goes too far."

"Look," I mumble. "I have no idea what I'm doing with my life. You know that about me. I haven't got much going on. But I do know that I look forward to seeing you."

"That's not a lot to build a relationship on," she says.

"I s'pose you're right, but it's all I've got right now."

"I need more than that. You need more than that. Listen, I've made some big mistakes. And just like it did the other day at Benji's, my past is going to come up. I can deal with it. I have and I will. But it's not your past. You don't know how to deal with it, and I'm not so sure you can, or that you should, or that I want you to."

"So that's it. Over before it starts."

"Better that way, don't you think?"

"No. I think I'd like to find out more."

"What, and then have it be over?"

"Why does it have to be over?"

"I'm sorry, but I've got a little girl to think about. I'm not interested in a short-term fling. You're sweet, but you just said it yourself, you don't know what you're doing with your life, and even if you did, it would be hard to be with someone who once sold her body, now wouldn't it?"

thirty-one

When we get back to Ruthie's there is an old silver Toyota in the drive. A dark-haired guy wearing a short beard hops out of it while two others turn their heads to look.

"Oh my God!" says Stephanie.

"What's the matter? What is it?"

"Just drop me off and then leave."

"Who is it?"

"Nobody. Just let me out."

"Not your husband?"

"Husband?" she glares at me. "I never had a husband. Not him."

"Samantha's dad?"

"Hey, babe!" the guy says.

"What do you want?" she says, getting out of the truck as Jasper hops out of the back.

"Just stopped by to say hello."

"Like hell. I thought you were in jail."

"Now that's no way to say hello," he says. "I got out early, and I came to see our daughter."

"She's not our daughter. She's my daughter. You stay the hell away from her. You don't even know her name."

"Well, it's been a long time since I've seen her—and you."

"You're not going to see her and now that you've seen me, hop in your car and you and your scumbag friends get out of here."

"Hey, babe, that's no way to talk to me—"

"What do you want, money?"

"No, it's not money, although I can always use a little more. It's you I've come to see."

"Get in the car and leave me alone, Sean."

"I've driven a long way—"

"She said leave," I say suddenly.

"Who asked you, town boy? Why don't you shut your mouth and go on home!"

"Danny, let me handle this."

"Yeah, Danny boy, let little Miss Stephanie handle this."

"Danny, please leave. Let me take care of this."

"That's right, Danny boy, get in your old farm truck and head home," he says as I head to the pickup.

"What the hell did I ever see in you?" says Stephanie.

"You know, babe, and I still got it for you."

"Shut your filthy—" she turns quickly when she sees Sean staring past her, and looks back at me. "Danny, no!"

"It's a clip-action, thirty-aught-six, shithead," I say, pointing the rifle directly at Sean. "Tell your buddies to get out of the car."

He does nothing.

"Now!" I yell.

Sean motions to his friends.

"Okay, tell them to put their hands on the hood of the car."

"Danny, are you crazy?"

"I know what I'm doing—now, punk, I'm going to tell you a little bit about this gun of mine. My father left it to me, and he took real good care of it, and so do I. So it'll fire just fine."

Bam!

Sean falls to the ground, covering up his head.

"The next time I pull the trigger, you won't hear the shot. What you will hear . . . well, I have no idea, and you won't be able to tell us. Now get your sorry ass back into your car and get the hell out of here."

But this doesn't really happen. This is just a story I imagine as I drive away. Because I do not do anything. I want to. But I do not. Jasper, on the other hand, did piss on the Toyota before we left.

thirty-two

The words from his mouth drift into my mind like the dust from the spinning tires of my truck. "Bye-bye, Danny boy, and take your stupid-ass dog with you!"

Stephanie is in the driveway, staring at me. Did I do what she wanted me to do? Or was I supposed to stay and have it out with Sean the way I imagined?

Billy is standing by a new black Honda SUV as I pull into my drive.

"Like it?" he says.

"It's nice," I say, my thoughts not on Billy or his new car.

"Just bought it."

"Nice," I repeat, still distracted.

"I quit."

"What?"

"I quit the park service."

"Why?"

"Couldn't do it anymore." I look into his eyes. We're the only family he seems to have. I never thought about him much before. Always, just an extra in our lives.

"Why weren't you at Benji's funeral?"

"I dunno. I guess I figured it would have been hypocritical."

"You shoulda been there."

"Maybe."

"Why did you tell the state about the letter?"

"What?"

"Why did you tell them about Benji's letter?"

Billy's mouth opens like a trout.

"Why'd you tell them?"

"You think I told them?"

"Yeah."

"After all these years—you don't know me very well."

"Did you?"

"No."

"Well, how'd they find out?"

"How the hell do I know? Besides, what's the big deal if they do know? Just because you and your father are probably the only ones to see the letter, it's not like other people don't know about it. It's worthless, anyway."

"How do you know?"

"If it wasn't worthless, Garrick would have done something by now."

"Well, the state didn't think it was worthless—Benji's dead because the state didn't think it was worthless."

"What are you talking about?"

"They went up there to find that letter, and Benji tried to stop them."

"You been listenin' to Garrick too much."

"Well, Benji didn't just fall. There was some kind of a fight."

"Now you're playing detective?"

"You know, Billy, you're right. All these years and I don't know you. I guess I never have."

"Maybe you never tried—anyway, I quit. And now I'm goin' away for a while."

"Whaddaya mean?"

"There's not a lot to keep me here."

"What about Mom?"

"You think I'm a fool?"

"What are you talking about?"

"I'm not stupid. All these years. Comin' over here, helpin' out. Pretending I was part of you guys." He shakes his head and looks down at the dirt on his boots. "Why I thought it would ever be different, I don't know."

Suddenly he looks up, his eyes looking deep into mine.

"You know the sad thing is, I really love her. I'd do anything for her—and for you. But it doesn't quite measure up. It would never measure up."

"What do you mean? Measure up to what?"

Billy chuckles. "To your father. Doesn't really matter, anyway. Your mother's never gonna marry me, right?"

"Why don't you ask me, not my son?"

Billy turns and looks at Mom, who's standing by the door on the porch.

"Okay, Linda," says Billy. "I'm right, aren't I?"

She looks long at him. "I gave my heart to one man," she says. "I can't lie to you and tell you that I could ever love you like I loved him."

"He was a great guy. To do what he did—"

My mother's eyes open wide, and Billy stops himself.

"I'm goin' away for a while. You change your mind, call me. I'll come back." He gets in the car. No handshake. No good-bye. Gone.

thirty-three

"What did he mean?"

"What?" says Mom.

"When he said, 'To do what he did'? What did he mean?"

"That," she says, smiling nervously. "Ah, to marry me. I was no catch."

"Don't tell me, you were pregnant before you guys got married?"

The nervous smile twitches.

"So I was a love child," I laugh. "What's the big deal? It happens to a lot of people."

As I walk by her, she reaches up to stroke my face. "You're so special," she says, tears filling her eyes. "So very, very special."

"What happens now?" I say.

"What do you mean?"

"No Billy."

"Well, we're going to have to figure out a way to fix things around here ourselves," she says with a laugh.

"What about you?" I say.

"Billy was right. I could never marry him. It needed to end some time. And what about you?"

"Me?"

"Yes, you and your young lady?"

"Stephanie?"

"She's very pretty."

"Yeah, well, we broke up, if we were ever going together."

"I'm sorry."

"No you're not, Mom."

"Well, okay, I'm not. You need to get on with your life. Go back to college."

"Yeah, maybe."

"She would have been—"

My look stops her. "Would have been what?"

"You don't need to get in a relationship now."

"That's pretty much what she said."

"Well, she's thinking sanely."

"Yeah, she probably is."

"Who's this?" Mom says, looking past me toward the end of the drive.

A state park ranger Jeep pulls into our dirt drive as a silver Toyota races past it. My eyes are on the Toyota as three men hop out of the Jeep: Pete, Billy's boss, and two in suits. One I know was at Benji's, but the other one I don't recognize.

"Hello, Linda," says Pete.

"Pete," Mom says curtly. "Billy just left, if you're looking for him."

"No, we're not looking for him. Actually, we've come to see Danny."

"Just want to ask him a couple of questions," says one of the suits. "May we come in?"

"Up to you, Danny," says Mom.

"Yeah, sure."

Mom opens the door.

"Mrs. Murtaugh, my name is Curtis Randazzo. I'm a criminal investigator for the state park service. I was at Mr. Samuels's house the other day. I take it you already know Pete Thompson. This is Russell Stevens," he says, introducing the other man in the suit. "Mr. Stevens is ah . . ."

"A special investigator with the city," Stevens says.

"Danny," says Randazzo, "we met on the day of Mr. Samuels's death."

"Right," I say. I follow them in.

Mom pulls a couple of wooden chairs from the kitchen into our tiny living room. I fall into the easy chair; the three men squish into the couch to my right. Mom sits on the piano bench across from me.

"The police are continuing their investigation, as you know," says Randazzo. "They think someone broke into Mr. Samuels's house, and he came in unexpectedly and surprised them. Mr. Samuels wasn't shot. It seems that he fell on the back steps and hit his head."

"That's probably when his gun went off, which is what you heard," says Pete.

"Well, what were these people looking for?" I say sarcastically. "It's not like Mr. Samuels had any money or anything valuable—or did he?" My sarcasm coats the conversation, and the men look at each other.

"Well, the best the police can figure is that whoever did this might have known that Benji had quite a collection of rifles and handguns," says Randazzo.

"The gun case was broken," says Pete, "but they weren't sure if anything was taken or not. I think the police may ask you if you remembered what was in the gun case, since you said you had been to his house before."

"How long had you known Mr. Samuels?" asks Stevens.

"Long enough," I say.

"But your father knew him," he says. "They were friends, right?"

"Yeah, that's what I've been told. My mother knows more about that than I do," I say.

"What's the point of your question?" says Mom.

"We're just trying to find out exactly what happened to Mr. Samuels," says Randazzo.

"I already told the police all I know. There's nothing more to add."

"Did Mr. Samuels ever mention a letter to you, Danny?" says Randazzo.

I don't answer.

"Did he?" he repeats.

"You need to answer the question, kid," says Stevens.

"How do you know about the letter?" I snap.

"Just answer the question," Stevens says.

Randazzo raises his hand slightly, stopping him. "Danny," Randazzo says quietly, "we know about the letter. It's common knowledge. We just want to know if Mr. Samuels talked to you about it. Did your husband ever mention it to you?" he asks, turning to Mom.

"I know about it," says Mom. "Like you said, it's common knowledge that Benji and Garrick had some kind of arrangement."

"Did either of you ever see it?" asks Randazzo.

"Whether we did or didn't, the letter's worthless. You killed Benji over a worthless piece of paper."

"What are you talking about?" says Randazzo.

"You guys went up there to find that letter. And when Benji tried to stop you, you got into a fight."

Stevens looks at the others and bursts out laughing.

"Kid, you're nuts!" says Stevens. "Where did you get that idea?"

"Garrick, no doubt," says Randazzo.

I turn and glare at him.

"I'd choose my friends more carefully," Stevens says.

"Danny," says Pete, "I know you're not going to buy this, but we're really trying to find out what happened up there."

"You're right, I don't buy it—why's he here?" I say, pointing to Stevens. "What's the city have to do with this?"

"He's—" says Pete, but Stevens cuts him off.

"Okay, kid, I'll lay my cards on the table," says Stevens.

Pete looks at him sharply.

"It's okay, Pete, everyone's going to know soon enough—it's about water," he says to me.

"Water?"

"Garrick's river is part of the city's watershed," says Pete.

"Yeah, so?"

Stevens shifts a little. "We've been in a drought for a while," he says.

I look at him, trying to follow, then it hits me. "You're gonna build a dam on his river?"

"You can't do that!" says Mom.

"I'm afraid they can," says Pete.

"You can't just take his river and build a dam," I say.

"If it means more water for millions of people—" says Stevens.

"Son of a bitch! You can't do that," I say.

"A dam," Mom whispers.

"It's just a job to you, isn't it?" I say to Stevens. "You don't really care about Garrick, his river. You don't even care about the millions of people and their drinking water. It's just a job."

His lips tighten.

"You know it's true. That's why you can't say anything. You got no heart. No passion. It doesn't mean diddly-shit to you."

"Did you see Benji's letter?" asks Pete.

"I thought you had it," I say.

"No, we don't," says Randazzo.

"Did you see it?" presses Stevens.

"What does it matter, anyway?"

"Well, if the city's going to move on this—" says Pete.

"There's no 'if,'" says Stevens. "It's just a matter of when."

"They need to know as much about any legal problems they might face as possible," Pete adds.

"So you came up here to ask me to help you? Fat chance. You wanna know what kinda problems you're gonna face. Well, you sure as hell can count on Frederick P. Garrick. He'll fight you every step of the way."

"This one's way over his head," says Randazzo.

"You think we'd do this without federal backing?" says Stevens. "Garrick is out of his league. We're going to take his river, and we're going to build a dam on it. End of discussion."

thirty-four

STATE CONDEMNS GARRICK LAND
FOR CITY WATER RIGHTS

City officials announced yesterday that they will begin condemnation proceedings against Frederick P. Garrick to create a much-needed reservoir. Citing increasing demand for water because of several years of light snowfall and summer drought, city officials, with state and federal aid, propose to construct a billion-dollar dam as a solution to ongoing water-supply problems.

"We don't wish to be in the business of building dams, but we will soon be in a desperate situation if we don't act quickly," said Russell Stevens, special assistant to the mayor.

Stevens said that the Garrick property is ideally situated to provide a back-up reservoir for city users. He added that the mayor has been in touch with state and federal authorities to acquire matching funds for the purchase of the Garrick property and the construction of the dam.

The city, the state, and the feds. Impressive. No mention of the letter. No mention of Benji's death. Very neatly done. Mr.

Garrick, I think they've got you this time.

"Shut up, you stupid dogs!" I yell at the Rottweilers, banging against the fence by the front door. "Mr. Garrick," I shout, opening the door after no one answers. I look back toward the garage. "His Jeep is here," I say aloud.

"Mr. Garrick!" I yell again, stepping cautiously inside. The sound of violins and French horns seep from the CD player into the yellowed wallpaper and old dark wood paneling. I look down at the small table standing by the door. His gun isn't there. "Mr. Garrick! It's me, Danny Murtaugh."

I walk slowly past the table with the maps of his land spread on them, past the pictures of Garrick and his grandfather with politicians and dignitaries. Past a newly framed eight-by-ten photo of the two rivers that I took from the overlook. Through the kitchen and out onto the screened-in back porch.

"Mr. Garrick," I say softly as I see a figure sitting by the opened porch door.

"Mr. Garrick," I repeat, even more quietly, as I step to the side of the old man, his uncombed white hair streaming past his large ears, a green and white Afghan draped over his knees, and the light brown handle and long blue stem of a .357 Magnum resting on his lap.

He looks really old. I never noticed just how old he is.

"Mr. Garrick," I say, whispering.

"I heard you the first time," says Garrick. "You have more pictures for me?"

"No, sir. I just thought I'd stop by and say hello."

"Well, you've said it."

I stand there waiting for an invitation to sit or to talk, but none comes.

"I just thought, maybe, you'd like someone to talk with," I say, breaking the long silence.

"About what?"

"About, well, about them condemning your land."

"Nothin' new."

"Well, they got the city and federal government involved now."

"So?"

"So—I don't know—" Suddenly the obvious escapes into the air. "Why don't you just sell them the land and be done with it?"

Frederick P. Garrick turns quickly toward me and looks up into my eyes. "I'm getting old, you know," he says, his stare not letting me look away or down. "No one gives a damn about this land but me." His eyes release me, and he looks toward the woods beyond the small clearing. "I've walked every inch of it. Every goddamned inch of it. And you know, it is goddamned." He turns back to me and waits until our eyes meet again, until he can be sure that I can't avoid his vision. "You know that?" he says to me, just like Benji did, when I was alone with him, and he was drunk. "Her beauty is so deep, it's demonic. Her love intoxicates you. The more you walk on her, the more she becomes your soul. And what do they want to do now? Flood her. Drown her. Suffocate her.

"I'm too old to stop them, but I'll be damned if I ever sell it to them." He turns his head away from me again. His thoughts drift across the early spring grass, melting into the dark and the deep of the forest. "I will not see it happen. I'll be dead before I see that happen."

I look down at the old man, the purple veins bulging and

pulsing in his neck, his hands trembling on his lap.

"Mr. Garrick, can I get you anything? A glass of water, maybe?"

Slowly he shakes his head no. "Go on, leave."

I walk back through the inner sanctuary of Garrick's world, step out onto the small stone front porch. One of the big Rottweilers raises its head and rolls its sad brown eyes.

BANG!

The dogs jump to their feet and jerk their heads toward the back of the house.

"Mr. Garrick! No!" I yell, racing inside to the screened-in porch, knocking over the maps. "No!" I turn the corner past the kitchen and step on the porch. The chair is empty.

"Mr. Garrick!" I yell.

"Got him!" yells the old man, standing on the edge of the grassy knoll, drenched in warm morning sunlight. "You'd think they'd learn by now not to mess with Frederick P. Garrick," he yells as he reaches down to pick up a dead woodchuck. "You would think they'd learn."

thirty-five

"Stephanie!" I say out loud as I see her walk into St. John's. And so for the third time in three weeks I walk into this church.

What is it that makes me so uncomfortable in a church, particularly a Catholic one? Is it the way the lights are turned down low so that all you can see are spots of candles burning in pockets for kneeling and praying, tucked away, so private, barely visible? Is it the smell of oldness—greasy, tattered books held in sweaty hands for generations, and sticky wooden slanted pews propping people up for years, decades, a century, and more? This church—every church?—is old in its very existence, crumbling, rotting, crying words, trying to stave off the stink of dying. That is why I cannot stand church. It's all about death, and none of them will admit it.

"May I help you?"

"No, I was just looking for someone," I say to the priest who stepped up behind me.

Stephanie—but it's not Stephanie—turns in the pew and looks at us.

"Oh," I mumble. "She's not, uh, it's not, uh, well, never mind."

"You're sure I can't help you?"

I stare at the man. "You're the priest who did Benji's service,"

I say.

"Yes. And you, I recall, are the very talented piano player who helped us out that day. Thank you, again."

"You're welcome. Glad to help. It was a nice service."

"I didn't know him at all, as I said that day, but many people did. I take it you were friends with him?"

"Well, not really. I only got to know him recently, but Stephanie and I found him when he was—when he died."

"Oh yes, now I remember, you're a friend of Stephanie and Ruth's. I met you, right, one Sunday?"

"Yeah."

"We talked a little about your father."

"You have a good memory."

"In my job it can be really embarrassing if I don't remember. Little things are important, like getting the names right at funerals and weddings."

The woman I thought was Stephanie walks by.

"See you Sunday, Father," she says.

The priest nods his head and turns back to me.

"Disappointed?" he says.

"Excuse me?"

"Not who you had hoped for."

"Uh, well, no."

"That's too bad, a person shouldn't be disappointed when they come to church."

"I don't think church had much to do with it."

"Depends on your point of view."

I hesitate. He continues.

"I mean, not a bad place to find a woman," he says, "—a church, that is."

"S'pose."

"Better than a bar."

"You have a point," I say.

"Of course, that depends on what your intentions are with the woman."

"There is that question, isn't there?"

"You'll meet some interesting women in a church, even if you didn't see the one you wanted."

Again, I pause. Again, he continues.

"Little old grandmothers, who are really quite courageous, you know. Every day they come to church and pray for others. Half crippled with arthritis. Some filling up with cancer. Catching their breath in between words. Every day they show up to pray for others. And there's other women, too. Blessed Kateri Tekakwitha," he says, pointing to a simple, stained-glass window of a young Indian woman. "She's one of the spiritual guardians of this area. She was orphaned by the Mohawks during a smallpox epidemic. And Saint Joan of Arc," he says, nodding to another stained-glass window, this one of a young girl bound at a stake looking upward. "The saint for our age, I think. Seventeen. Could neither read nor write. Betrayed by her own people, she sat before dozens of cardinals, bishops, and church clerics—hypocritical, pompous, and false—for days on end, and told the truth. She was willing to die for the truth. An amazing woman. We could all use a bit more of her in our lives."

Then he motions to follow him to one of those burning-candle alcoves, this one in the back of the church.

"And, of course, the most wonderful of all women, Mary," he says, his eyes turning intently to a picture of a dark-skinned woman dressed in a light blue robe and surrounded by gold.

"This is a painting of Our Lady of Guadalupe. She appeared to Juan Diego in Mexico with a message of hope."

I nod politely, not knowing what else to do. The windows and the painting made sense to him, were important to him. But they didn't mean much to me—except, maybe, they all seemed sad—but then again, maybe not sad.

"I hope I have not offended you," he said, aware of my nervousness.

"Uh, no, no, you haven't. They're, uh, nice."

He laughs slightly. "Yes, they are indeed nice."

"Here," he says, picking up a small, postcard-size picture of the lady in the painting. "You might find this helpful. On the back is a prayer. It's called a litany to Our Lady of Guadalupe."

Again, I hesitate.

"If you don't like it, you can throw it away. You won't go to hell—I don't think," he says with a laugh. "And it might possibly be of some use to you in your search for that right woman. To me, this describes the perfect woman. I don't think we should settle for less. Do you? Of course, that means we have to be worthy of her. And that is a problem."

Mother of the rejected.

I slide the little card with the picture of the sad Mary into my shirt pocket.

thirty-six

"Hey, you becoming religious?"

I turn around into the hard stare of Ruthie. She draws in a long breath of smoke from the cigarette hanging from her mouth. She pulls the thing away and studies it a moment. "I should really give these up, you know," she says. "So what does bring you into our church's parking lot?"

"Nothing. Just talking with the priest."

"Really?"

"Yeah, really."

"Lookin' for advice?"

"Not particularly."

"From Father Stephen, not me."

"Like I said, not particularly."

"Don't suppose you want any from me."

"Haven't you given me some already? 'Don't get involved,' I think it was."

"Yes, I suppose I did say that. You didn't listen."

"No, I guess I didn't."

"Stephanie told me what happened with Sean. You did the right thing."

"Didn't feel like it."

"Still and all, you did the right thing. Be careful of him. He's crazy."

"Yeah, well, I can take care of myself."

"Typical guy. I know you don't want my advice, but I'm giving it anyway—go back to college."

"And leave your niece alone?"

"Yeah, that's part of it. She's had a hard life. She's just getting back on her feet—"

"And she doesn't need to be involved. We've been through this."

"Not completely. Let me ask you this, you have any intention of marrying her?"

"What are you talking about? We barely know each other. I've only kissed her once."

Ruthie's frown stops me.

"Well, the truth is, she kissed me, if you must know. One kiss is hardly grounds for getting married."

"True, but one kiss leads to another, and another, and a lot, and then kids. Doesn't make you bad or her bad; just a fact. Now here's another fact. You're a pretty boy, a talented boy, a smart boy, a boy whose future isn't here in this town. It's out there," she says, swinging her arm like Benji did in the forest, out around him at the great majesty of nature. "Your life is out there. Are you planning on taking along a young woman with a little girl and a large past? If not, then I say again: don't get involved," she says, throwing the cigarette onto the ground and grinding it into the gravel beneath her shoe.

She starts to walk away.

"I don't know what I'm planning," I say to her. "I don't know—"

"You should know what you stand for first," she says, turning back to me. "Then you can plan. Your problem is that you don't know what you stand for. It's too bad your father isn't alive. He knew what he stood for."

"Keep my dad out of this."

Ruthie's eyes narrow, like two dams holding back hot lava.

"Listen, you little bastard, you would do well to know what your father would do!"

"He's none of your business!"

"The hell he isn't. My niece is my business, and anything to do with her is my business. That means you and your father and your mother, because your father knew what was right no matter what the cost."

"You don't have to tell me that. I know that better than you do. I was there when he dove into the river to save that god-damned dog! You weren't there, you son of a bitch! Not you, not anyone, just me. So don't tell me about my father!"

"Well, here's another piece of information about your father, something that you probably never heard! And maybe if you listen you might find out why your dad went into that river to save that stupid dog. Maybe it'll help you understand what kind of a man he was and what kind of a man he wanted you to be. Maybe you ought to stop runnin' from him and find out who he was.

"So for just a moment, try to listen," she says, catching her breath. "Back in high school, I was a senior. Your dad and mom were seniors, too. Benji was kinda in special classes. He was supposed to be a senior, but I don't know if he really was. Billy was in tenth grade. It was the summer after graduation. A bunch of us graduates and Ryan Garrick were hanging around down at the pool."

"Old man Garrick's younger brother?"

"Yeah."

"What was he doing there?"

"He used to come around during summertime. They were half brothers. Ryan was a lot younger than his brother. Mostly he hung out and drank with us. Your mom used to date him once in a while."

"You're kidding!"

"She never told you that?"

"No. She said she knew him some, that's about it."

"Well, she knew him more than some. They used to date. I think maybe to get your dad jealous.

"So there we are this one day, and around the corner comes Benji carrying something. Hands outstretched in front of him, balancing something carefully. He sees Billy and says to him, 'Billy, I was lookin' for ya. Here, I want to show you something,' and he brings over this case of trout flies that he had tied. He was so proud of it.

"Billy looks around to see how he's suppose to act. And we're all, you know, smiling, snickering, making fun of Benji. So he turns to Benji and says something like, 'What makes you think I care what you've got, you moron.'

"Benji is devastated. Mutters something like, 'I thought you'd like to see what I done.'

"Somebody says something like, 'Have done, you idiot, look what I have done.'

"Pretty soon we're all making fun of him. His face is getting redder and redder. He looks at Billy to help him, but Billy just starts laughing, too. I didn't say anything, and neither did your mom, but I didn't stop it, either.

"One of the guys flicks him on the ear, and when he turns to see who did it, he drops the case and the flies spill all over the place. As he bends down to pick them up, someone sticks one of the flies on his rear end. Then there's a mad scramble, and pretty soon they're all sticking him with flies. His butt, his arms, his legs, even his neck. He's covered with them, and it's not just on his clothes; they're stickin' them into his skin. He starts swinging his arms crazylike, but he can't stop them and he falls to his knees. By this time your mother is yelling for them to stop it, but no one is paying any attention, they're all just yellin' and laughin'. And then suddenly your dad rounds the corner. He stands there staring at what's goin' on.

"Then he says, 'Leave him alone.' A guy named Vince, who was the captain of the football team, says to him, 'Who's gonna make me?' This guy was about six-foot-three and weighed around 230 pounds. Your dad, well, you know, your dad wasn't big. All of about five-eight, and he couldn'a weighed more than 140. But he walks up to Vince, looks him in the eye, and says, 'I said, leave him alone.'

"Vince tries to grab your dad, and, well, it took about thirty seconds. Your father hit him about fifteen times really fast—I'd never seen anything like it. Then he turned to the rest of us, and said, 'Pick up his flies,' which we did. He took Benji out to his pickup truck. Benji's mom and dad had both passed away, and I think he was probably mostly living with Garrick. So it was probably Garrick that your dad took him to."

"What about Mom?"

"Your mother? Well, that was the last time she ever went out with Ryan Garrick or hung out with any of us. She and your dad got married in the fall."

"And I came along soon after."

"Yeah, guess you did."

thirty-seven

"Hey, Mom, I'm home," I yell. "Mom?"

"In here," comes a voice muffled in tears.

"What's the matter?"

She looks up, her legs draped over the old easy chair in the corner next to the couch, covered with old photos.

"After all these years, I still miss him," she whispers. "I will always miss him. That's why I can't marry Billy. Could never. I hurt him, Billy, you know." She's holding the photo of Dad with Benji and Billy.

"I took those from Benji's house the other day," I tell her, nodding toward Benji's old photos. "He said I could have them after he died. Didn't think it would be so soon—I didn't know that you and Garrick's brother dated."

Her head snaps up. "What?"

"Ruthie told me."

"What'd she say?"

"Nothin' really. No need to get upset."

"What'd she tell you?"

"Mom, what's the matter?"

She stands up in front of me.

"What did she tell you?" she demands.

"She told me a story about Benji and you and Garrick's

brother and her, and that Dad beat the crap out of some football player. She said you used to date Garrick's brother, then you and Dad got married. Then I came along."

She falls back in the chair. I look at her, crumpled up like a pile of laundry.

"You didn't—" I start to say. "You and Garrick's brother. You didn't—My God, he's not my father, is he?"

She shakes her head. "No," she says.

"How do you know?"

"I know. He's not your father."

"All this time, is that why you didn't want me to be up on Garrick's land, to see Benji? It's all about this? You thought I'd find out about all this?"

"You didn't need to know any of this."

"Mom, I still don't get it. What's the big deal?"

She stares at me.

"What is it?"

"Garrick thought, and probably still thinks, that you're his brother's son. When your dad died, he insisted that he help take care of you—anonymously. I let him. You have no rich grandfather."

"What?"

"Garrick paid for all those trips to the city."

"This is too much," I say, turning to stare out of the bay window to the field beyond.

The flies are what catch my eye. A swarm of them. They hover and dive and sit on something in the field near the house.

"What's that?" I say, pointing to flies on the thick yellow thing. "Jasper!" I scream, racing from the house.

I beat the air, swinging wildly at the fat little wings of

death.

"Mom! Mom! It's Jasper!

"You're going to make it!" I whisper to him, his body rising and falling, the blood pouring out of his side with every heave. I pick him up and carry him toward the porch.

"Mom!"

The door swings open.

"Oh my God! What happened?"

"I think he's been shot."

Mom stares at me.

"Call the vet!"

thirty-eight

I pull into a parking space across the street from the old silver Toyota as the three of them walk out from one of the bars.

I jump out of my pickup and charge across the street.

Sean says something to his buddies, but I'm on him before they say anything back. I slam my body into him. My left arm round his waist, the right clawing at his face. I smash him against the brick building. My left hand crunching and scraping against the wall, as I drive him into the front of the bar. My right hand, first a fist, jolts his head back, again and again, then it grabs tightly around his throat. Now I'm on top, my fingers squeezing into the flesh, tightening their grip on his larynx. His mouth open, gagging, choking, dying.

Thud!

A boot full in my face and now I'm on my back, squirming like a turtle rolled to its shell.

Thud! Thud! Thud! My face, my stomach, my chest. My breath, a thing I lunge for, but it's outside me. He's standing over me now.

A slice of silver glimmering in the spring sunshine hangs in his hand. His buddies have me pinned to the ground. I kick, I twist, I squirm, I cry.

"You're dead!" he screams. "Dead!"

He's over me. The spit and the blood drooling down his face. No smile. No satisfaction. Just pure hatred. Pure hatred for me, like me for him.

Squealing tires! People screaming! Car doors slamming!

Thunk! His head snaps forward. Eyes clamp shut. Knees buckle. He crumples to the ground.

Their hands let go. I roll to my stomach and struggle to my knees.

In the middle of the people all around, Billy lowers his rifle slowly to his side and kneels beside me.

"You okay?" he says quietly.

I nod my head yes. "How did you—"

"Your mom. She thought you'd do something stupid."

thirty-nine

"Full mobility? Probably not. There are a lot of bones in a hand," the doctor is saying. "If you were younger, maybe. But at your age, it won't ever be what it was, even with the best surgery and rehab."

I look at my mother, who's trying not to cry.

"I'm sorry, Mom."

"You're alive. That's all that matters."

I look down at the cast on my left hand.

"You'll be able to play, but—"

"But limited, right?" I ask.

"It'll be limited, yes."

"Sorry," I say again as I slide into the passenger's side of the pickup.

"Why do you keep saying 'Sorry'? Sorry for what? It's not your fault," she says.

I turn my head to her, and suddenly it hits me. "Then whose fault is it?"

"What?"

"Whose fault is it?" I repeat.

"What do you mean?"

"I mean, whose fault is it that life turns out the way that it does?"

"It's not anybody's fault."

"I think it is. I think it has to be."

"What are you talking about?"

"Don't you see? Don't you get it? There has to be a fault. Someone, somehow has to be at fault. There has to be a wrong that set all this in motion. Otherwise," I whisper to myself, "there's no right. And then there's no point, and there has to be a point.

"Drop me off at St. John's," I say suddenly. "I wanna talk to that priest. He's gotta know. If anyone should know, he should know."

"You can't go in and see a priest. Look at you. You're covered in blood. You just broke your hand. You were almost killed. You're going home to rest."

"Mom, all my life I've been avoiding this—I've been hiding in my piano, in my fantasy world. Running away from who I am. Running away from Dad's death. All this time, my life has been postponed—until some point in the future. The future has changed. My hand is broken. Smashed up in a fight with a guy who killed my dog. What've I been doing? Wandering around Old Man Garrick's woods taking pictures. Garrick knows what he's got—or what's got him. Me, I don't know anything but this," I say, holding up my broken hand. "All of this that's happened, well, it's somebody's fault. And I'll betcha that priest knows whose fault it is. So pull around the corner and drop me off."

forty

In one of those candle alcoves, with the light flickering with every breath this building breathes, sits a small statue of Jesus. It's not like other statues that I've seen of Him, not that I've seen that many, not that I ever really cared. He's stretched out so thin on this metal cross that His arms are just muscles and tendons, like rubber bands about to break. His head hangs down resting on His chest, and His rib cage sticks out like bare branches on a winter tree. But what gets me is this: the blood gushing from His side like vomit.

Whose fault is that?

The priest isn't here today. No one is. Like my father, I would rather be outside in the world trying to wrestle with the questions I have rather than stuck inside a church with candles, dancing to every thought passing my attention. But I'm the one who walked in here. I'm the one who thought I'd find something inside.

"Whose fault is it that things have turned out this way?" I say.

"Danny," a soft whisper floats through the candlelight.

"Stephanie. What are you doing here?"

"Your mom came and got me. She thought you might need someone to talk to."

"I get claustrophobic, you know," I say, looking around the church.

Stephanie slides her hand into mine and kneels. I follow her slowly to my knees.

We stay there in silence. Her eyes close, and I close mine. Then she makes the sign of the cross, stands up, and says, "Okay, let's go to your church."

forty-one

"It's breathtaking," says Stephanie.

"The river's low now, but if you look closely you can see the current of Garrick's river. See how it collides with the main river when it hits it? See the whitecaps of the rapids out there in the middle? They're a bitch to try to canoe through, because you have two currents fighting, and one of them is coming at you from the side."

"Wouldn't want to be out there today," she says, shivering, as spring winds whistle through the evergreens.

"The water temperature in April is still very cold, even if we didn't have much snow. Fall in on a chilly day in April and you'd probably die from hypothermia."

"I can't swim," she says with a laugh, "so it wouldn't matter if it was warm or cold, I'd be dead."

I turn away.

"What is it? What did I say? Oh my—down there's where it happened, isn't it?"

I say nothing.

"I'm so sorry. I didn't realize."

"The first time I came here," I say, walking toward the edge, "you know what I thought about? Jumpin'. It's about two hundred feet down. But it's not that easy to do. You know, the ledge slopes some, so it wouldn't be a clean jump. I think you'd get tangled in the trees. Probably break some bones, but I'm not so sure you'd die. So you'd have a lot of pain, but you'd still be alive."

I turn back to Stephanie. "My life has taken some interesting twists and turns in the last week or so," I say, laughing slightly. "And I end up here, looking at where it all started. With still no answers. You know why I went into the church?"

"I suppose to try to find some answers."

"Yeah. But do you know what the question was, is?"

"No."

"Whose fault is it? I looked at Jesus hanging on a cross, and I asked myself, Him, 'Whose fault is that?' I didn't get an answer. Now I look out at this river, at where my father died, when I was nine years old, and I wonder whose fault that was. And I think somehow it's all my fault.

"We were just going for a walk to see how high the river was. It had poured for twelve hours straight. I mean poured. I think they said we got eight inches of rain in twelve hours that day. It was September. School had just started. The storm was the leftover of some hurricane, but it stalled over us. And it just rained and rained.

"We walked close to the water's edge in the flat over there," I say, pointing to the far side of the big river. "All that was underwater. We were standing up by that big white sycamore in the distance. Not the one close to the river. No, the big one standing by itself in that field. That's how high the river was. We were watching all the debris. Huge branches and even trees were bobbing for their lives in the river. Then I saw the dog. It was just a head, straining, struggling, scratching to stay up. Coming at us from Garrick's river. I yelled, 'Dad, there's a dog out there.' He had seen it, too. 'Do something! Do something! You've got to go get it!' I yelled at him.

"He was already taking his shoes off by then. He tore off his shirt, and I heard him say, 'If I can get out there . . .' He was pointing to where you see that big rock. 'If I can get out there, I can catch him.' Then he went in.

"He made it to the dog. It was amazing. He actually made it to the dog, and then he started back with it. They went under but came back up. The current was pulling them downstream fast. I ran down the side of the river to meet them. He pulled the dog into a little eddy, down there, and they both stumbled over the slippery rocks, falling every so often in the shallow water. Then he crawled up onshore. He looked at me and smiled. 'Made it, son.' Those were his last words. They said it was a heart attack."

Stephanie reaches her hand to mine.

"You can't blame yourself," she is saying, like so many other people had said to me, so many dozens of times before. "You said he was already taking off his shoes by the time you had said anything."

I look into her deep green eyes.

"There's more, isn't there?" she says.

I look away, because I can't look at her and say the one thing that I've been wanting to say all these years, the one thing I have never said to anyone, even to myself.

"When my father died, all I thought about was the dog. My father was dying, and I called the dog over and started to pet it. I didn't hold his hand. I didn't touch him. I couldn't. I couldn't even touch him when he was dying. I looked away and stroked the head of some goddamned dog. And my father died without me holding him, talking to him, telling him that I loved him. My God, my God, please forgive me!"

forty-two

It has been about a year since then. The cast came off my wrist and hand, and in the fall, I went back to school. Stephanie thought it best that we not have much contact, and so we haven't.

The bullet the vet dug out of Jasper's side matched a handgun that Sean had. It was one of Benji's.

Garrick is still fighting over the land, but there's not much of a fight anymore. Seems not everyone in the federal government was in favor of giving the city money to build a dam. And then suddenly it started to rain. All summer; all fall. The rain turned into snow, the worst winter in thirty years. And this spring it's still raining. The reservoirs have been full for months. Garrick's land will not be taken by the city for a reservoir. We have a new governor who simply fired the director of parks and recreation for spending too much money on buying new land and not taking care of the parks the state already owned. Frederick P. Garrick was right after all. Garrick will probably die on his land. But he still fights. He will always fight. It's what gives him meaning, I think.

I keep to myself, too. College is like a job—a temporary job. I still don't know what the future holds. I play the piano; it's part of my job. I will never be a great master. The bones in my left hand did not all heal perfectly. Sometimes the music gives me something, often it doesn't. And so a year later, it's spring break again. Mom tells me Stephanie, Samantha, and Ruthie are moving. So here I am driving to say good-bye to the one person who knows me in ways that no one else does, no one else could.

"Hey, college boy," says Ruthie, opening the door. "Come on in. We got company, Steph!" she hollers upstairs.

Samantha is sitting at a piano, plunking keys.

"Starting her early, huh," I say to Ruthie.

"You want a cup of coffee?"

"Sure, if you've got some ready."

"Any ex-drunk always has coffee ready. How do you want it?"

"Regular. Cream and sugar. Spread your fingers out," I say to Samantha as I slide onto the bench next to her.

"Put your thumb over this key," I say, pointing to middle C. "This one's called C. Now press your thumb down on it. Good. You just played C."

"I'll just set the coffee on the table," says Ruthie, sitting down to watch.

"Thanks. Now press your next finger on the next key. That one's called D. That's it. And now your middle finger. That's E. Then the next. That's F. And then the pinky. That's G. Very good. Very good."

"You're a teacher, huh?"

"What? This?"

Ruthie raises her eyebrows and nods. "Yeah, this."

"Well, to tell you the truth, I've thought about it before."

"You'd be good at it."

"Thanks."

"Hey."

I turn to the voice. She stands there, dressed like she was at Benji's that night in a spring long ago. Pink blouse, rolled-up sleeves, blue jeans. Her curls falling about her shoulders, her green eyes piercing.

She wraps her arms around me. I've longed for this moment so desperately. I think I will die for what I feel for her. I want to tell her that, but I know it is not right. I don't know why, but to tell her would not be fair to her. It would only be about me.

"So, how are you?" Stephanie says as she pulls away.

"I'm doing fine," I say. "Mom told me she heard you're movin'."

"Yeah, I got accepted at the university."

"Great."

"Single mom and all. They've got scholarships available, I guess."

"That, and straight As," adds Ruthie.

"Good for you," I say. "Well, anyway, I thought I'd stop by to say good-bye."

"Wanna go for a walk?" she says.

"Sure. That'd be nice."

She grabs my hand, and I realize how lonely I have been, not just this past year, but my whole life.

In the midday of spring, with a hot sun showering us with warmth, we walk along the side of a dirt road. A few early red and yellow tulips bend in the breeze against the bright yellow backdrop of forsythia and daffodils. Birth and rebirth, and beauty all around. She is so stunning, her curls blowing lightly on her neck and face. Her eyes smile; she takes my hand, squeezes it, and so we walk, until walking turns awkward and silence becomes unbearable.

"What are you thinking?" I say.

"What it would have been like if you and I had met when we were younger."

"Would it have been different?"

"I don't know. I suppose we couldn't have met. We weren't ready to meet each other. What are you thinking?" she says.

"How beautiful you are."

"You're always sweet."

"I can't let you go."

"You have no choice."

Her eyes are wet, and her soft kiss on my cheek says that the end is near.

"I have something for you back at the house," she whispers.

Every step we take, I take alone. And then we're in the living room again, Samantha still at the piano.

"Here," she says, handing me an envelope as she walks me to the porch. "I think this might help you understand."

And then, for the second time in my life, I was kissed by her, full on the lips, and if I ever fall in love, I will know what to judge it by. It will have to be better than that kiss.

I am sitting at home now. Mom bought another yellow Labrador pup, and he's chewing on my shoelaces as I read what Stephanie wrote.

My dearest Daniel,

I do not know for sure why I cannot be with you, but for now it must be so. I thought of you often this past year, and thought more than once to call you, but I knew in my heart it would be disastrous for both of us. You awoke something in me long dead, and perhaps I did the same for you. These words by Saint Augustine capture it for me, perhaps for you, too:

Late have I loved you, O Beauty, so ancient and so new, late have I loved you! And behold, you were within me and I was outside, and there I sought for you, and in my deformity I rushed headlong into the well-formed things that you have made. You were with me, and I was not with you. Those outer beauties held me far from you, yet if they had not been in you, they would not have existed at all. You called, and cried out to me and broke open my deafness;
. . . I tasted, and I hunger and thirst; you touched me, and I burned for your peace.

May you find Peace.
Love always,
Stephanie

"Danny?"

"Yeah, Mom,"

"It's Father Stephen on the phone for you."

"Father Stephen?"

Mom raises her eyebrows and shakes her head. "I have no idea," she says, handing me the phone.

"Danny," he says.

"Yes."

"I heard you were home."

"Yeah, spring break."

"Will you be here in town this summer?"

"Probably. I'm not exactly sure, but probably."

"I know this question I'm about to ask is way out of left field, but, well, Margaret, our organist, passed away suddenly. Well, I was just wondering—"

"How did you know I was home?"

"Stephanie—"

"So you're wondering if—"

"Well, I know it's a lot to ask. Just till we find someone else."

I look down at the note in my hand—moments on moments on moments. You touched me, I read to myself, and I burned for your peace.

I smile at the thought of sitting in a church playing for people who can't sing, and I remember her next to me, so sweet, so holy, so pure, and Benji's coffin and the Christ on the cross on the wall beyond us both—be still, my soul. Be still.

"Sure, why not."